P9-CFD-308

Praise for

The Curious Cats Spy Club

"A fun mystery series that's a sure bet for animal lovers."
—*School Library Journal*

"This first book in a new series is definitely for the animal-lover, and the Scooby-Doo vibe makes it a perfect fit for the budding mystery fan. Young readers will enjoy following the clues along with Kelsey as she learns about friendship and animals."—*Booklist*

"There's plenty of action in this series opener, but Singleton also handles the emotional layers well. Pet lovers will enjoy the animal-centric focus, and the mystery will keep them guessing."—*Publishers Weekly*

"This enjoyable mystery has a satisfying ending and a neatly calibrated level of suspense."—*Kirkus Reviews*

"This is a feel-good book with a myriad of unexpected twists, turns, and surprises."—*VOYA*

"Ultimately as fuzzy and accessible as a kitten chasing a ball of string, this story—and subsequent titles in the series—will likely find a ready audience among animal lovers, amateur sleuths, and the fairly common combination of the two."
—*Bulletin of the Center for Children's Books*

The Curious Cat Spy Club Mysteries

The Curious Cat Spy Club
The Mystery of the Zorse's Mask
Kelsey the Spy
The Secret of the Shadow Bandit

The Curious Cat Spy Club #4

Book Four
The Secret of
the Shadow Bandit

Linda Joy Singleton

Albert Whitman & Company
Chicago, Illinois

This book is dedicated to the juvenile series
book collecting community who will recognize
the series books tropes woven into this mystery.

Special thanks to Jennifer Fisher, president of the
Nancy Drew Sleuths fan club and publisher of the
Sleuth fanzine, and to Garrett Lothe, publisher of
the *Susabella Passengers and Friends*—two great
juvenile series book publications that celebrate
series books for young (and young at heart) readers.

Library of Congress Cataloging-in-Publication
data is on file with the publisher.

Text copyright © 2016 by Linda Joy Singleton
Published in 2016 by Albert Whitman & Company
ISBN 978-0-8075-1385-9

Printed in the United States of America
10 9 8 7 6 5 4 3 2 1 LB 20 19 18 17 16

Cover illustration by Lora Lee
Interior illustrations and hand lettering by Jordan Kost
Design by Ellen Kokontis

For more information about Albert Whitman & Company,
visit our web site at www.albertwhitman.com.

Contents

Three Months Ago...

RJ peered up into the dense leaves of the towering oak tree. Opening his palm, he held up raisins and called softly, "Bandit!"

He heard a rustling sound overhead and saw a flash of a gray tail.

RJ couldn't see the small animal's face, but he knew Bandit's black eyes would be shining. He'd found out the best foods to feed his semi-wild animal from reading online and talking to a veterinarian. Fruit, veggies, and meat were good. Not too much sugar, though, as Bandit's teeth could get cavities. Bandit wasn't fully grown. She was a teenager like him—in animal years anyway. When he found her half-dead in a ditch, she had an indentation around her neck like she'd recently worn a collar.

Bandit wasn't the only wild creature he'd nursed back to health. There was the bunny with the bleeding foot that he and his friends had found when they were exploring the woods behind the cottage, a baby bird that had fallen out of its nest, and a lizard that was nearly frozen to death. His friends helped, of course, but RJ discovered he had a natural talent for healing. So he read about animal science and James Herriot's stories of being a country vet. RJ couldn't wait to be old enough to go to college and study to become a veterinarian.

Smiling at the image of himself in a white doctor's coat with a waiting room of people and their pets, RJ climbed through the trap door into the tree house.

A furry head peeked out from a tiny hole in the wall. Bandit hesitated, still wary of humans. While RJ waited for her to come inside, he set the table with three sodas, three fruit snack packets, and plastic silverware.

Out of the corner of his eye, RJ saw furry paws scamper toward him. He held out the raisins to

Bandit. Her whiskers were inches from his fingers when he heard a squeal of tires and a slammed car door.

RJ bumped over a chair as he rushed to the window.

Why was his dad home so early?

Climbing to the ground, RJ glanced up and saw Bandit peering down at him from a gnarled branch.

His father stomped over with an expression so hot with rage that RJ drew back. He felt like he was looking at a stranger instead of his easy-going, soft-spoken father. "Go inside the house and pack!"

Then his father told him something so horrible that RJ gasped like he'd been punched in the gut. Stunned, he barely noticed when the raisins fell from his hand to the ground.

Only when his father went into the house did he look back up into the tree.

Of course timid Bandit was gone.

And soon RJ was gone too.

- Chapter 1 -
Monstrous

A shrill scream rips through the house.

I jump off the window seat, fling my mystery novel aside, race out of my bedroom and—*Wham!*—into the solid mass of big brother.

"Whoa, Kelsey!" Kyle's hair is mussed like he just woke up from a nap. He puts his hands on my shoulders and peers into my face. "Why'd you scream?"

"Not me...Kiana, I think," I say as another scream echoes through the hall. I whirl around and run into her room, my brother close on my heels.

My older sister is perched on her bed, clutching a stuffed pink bunny to her chest like a shield. "Get the monster out of here!" she shrieks.

"What monster?" Kyle scrunches his forehead, looking around.

"It moved too fast to get a good look, but I think it's a fanged snake or horned lizard with a spiky tail," Kiana says in a rush.

A fanged horned monster with a spiky tail?

I want to believe Kiana because she's nicer to me than Kenya and sometimes she even helps me with my homework. But there's no monster in her room.

"It's in my closet!" Kiana points a shaky finger. "I saw a horrifying shadow on the wall then heard claws running into my closet so I kicked the door shut. It's still there!"

"You only saw a shadow?" Kyle scoffs. "Don't you know that shadows are always more exaggerated than reality? I'm not surprised you're imagining monsters after you and Kenya stayed up late watching *Jurassic Park*."

"That has nothing to do with this...this *creature*!" Kiana squeals, her gaze glued to the closet. "I came into my room to get my backpack and heard a crunching sound—and look! That *thing* chewed my book report!" Kiana picks up a shredded paper from her bed and waves it at us.

I stare at needle-sharp punctures and clawed

stripes, and my stomach knots. As Spy Tactics Specialist in the Curious Cat Spy Club, I've trained myself to observe and analyze evidence. The claw and teeth marks are proof I can't ignore. A horrible suspicion grows in my mind.

"A monster ate your homework?" Kyle throws back his head and laughs. "Try getting that excuse by your teacher."

"It's true! And it's probably devouring my clothes and best shoes right now!" Kiana twists a curl of her dark hair around her finger. "Hurry, Kyle! You're older and stronger than we are. Get rid of it!"

My brother's smile fades fast. While he's tall and can play a mean game of hoops, he's not made of muscles or courage. And lately he's been too busy researching colleges to play any sports. He glances uneasily at the closet, backing into the hall like he's poised for a quick getaway. "I'll go ask Mom to help. Catching animals is her job, so she'll know what to do."

"She's working in the garden," Kiana says.

"No need to bother Mom on her day off," I say calmly even though my heart is thudding. I step forward. "I'll do it."

My brother and sister stare at me, shocked. I'm the youngest in the family after all, the little sister who's usually so quiet no one notices me. They probably think I'm trying to prove I can be brave, but my offer has nothing to do with bravery. It's the opposite. If my suspicion about the "monster" is right, I'm going to be in big trouble. My only hope is to get my sister and brother out of the room.

"I can handle this." I imagine I'm a fearless detective from one of my novels and lift my chin confidently. "I've learned a lot about dealing with wild animals from hanging out with Becca at her wild animal sanctuary. Alligators, lions, and bears—they don't scare me. Becca's taught me how to protect myself, but I can't protect both of you, so wait in the hall."

Kiana frowns at her ripped homework then jumps off her bed and comes over to me. "I can't leave you in here alone," she says anxiously.

"Really, it's okay. Don't worry."

As I say this I hear rustling sounds from the closet and wonder what will happen if I'm wrong. Could there really be a spiked-tail snake-lizard in the closet?

"Kelsey knows a lot about wild animals, so she can take care of this," my brother says with a shrug. "Come on, Kiana. Let's get out of here."

"But Kelsey could get hurt." She tugs my hand. "Better my shoes get eaten than my baby sister. Let's all leave and go get Mom."

"Get Mom to do what?"

I spin around as Mom strides into the room. Her curly brown hair falls out of a red scarf and her gardening gloves are dirt-stained. Before she became a county animal control officer, she worked for a florist because she loves gardening.

I wish she'd stayed outside in the garden.

Things get worse when I hear Kenya's and Dad's voices.

Drats! Now my whole family is here.

"What's going on?" Dad squeezes in beside Mom. He must have been in the kitchen working on a culinary masterpiece because he's wearing his *Eating Is a Necessity but Cooking Is an Art* apron.

"Kiana, did you scream?" Kenya pushes past everyone to hug her. They both have long dark-brown hair like Mom's and full lips like Dad, and everyone says they're identical. But I can tell them apart. It's Secret 8 in my notebook of secrets.

"Mom, Dad!" Kiana gestures wildly. "There's a monster in my closet!"

Dad wipes his hands on his cooking apron as he chuckles. "Aren't you a little old for imaginary friends?"

"It's not a friend or imaginary! See what it did to my book report!" Kiana waves the ripped homework in the air. A corner breaks off and flutters to the carpet.

Mom pushes her hair from her eyes, leaning in for a closer look at the paper. "Hmmm," she murmurs. "What does this monster look like?"

"Horrifying! It was huge like a giant lizard or dragon with wicked fangs!" Kiana spreads her arms and juts out her teeth like fangs. "And it had a spiky tail!"

"But you only saw its shadow," I point out, hoping to calm everyone down and convince them to leave. "I'm sure it's just a harmless rat. I can get rid of it."

"No, you will not, Kelsey," Mom says firmly as she steps in front of me. "Rats carry diseases. Kyle, go out to my work truck and grab my net."

We all wait as if frozen in a movie frame. Kiana and Kenya stand close, their hands dramatically clasped together and their gazes fixed on the closet door like they're actors in a horror movie. Dad stands by awkwardly like an extra, while Mom waits to direct the action.

Minutes later, Kyle's footsteps pound down the hall and he hands Mom the net before he quickly ducks back into the hall.

Mom raises the net in one hand, reaching for the closet with the other.

I hold my breath as Mom twists the knob.

Slowly, the door opens...

- Chapter 2 -
Houdini Cat

"Stand back, kids," Mom warns.

The others huddle in the hall, but I step forward to look inside the closet.

Just as I feared, I recognize the "monster."

Of course, there's nothing monstrous about my sweet kitten. Honey is adorable with long marmalade-colored fur, white patches across her back, and a stubby tail that's twitching as if she's annoyed.

"Honey!" I rush forward to scoop up my cat. She mews with attitude, letting everyone know she does not appreciate being locked in a closet.

"Some terrifying monster." Mom chuckles, the net dangling from her hand.

Kyle swaggers into the room. "I thought the monster had a spiked tail."

"It did!" Kiana waves her arms emphatically. "It can't be a kitten!"

"You only saw its shadow." Kyle smirks. "I can't believe you freaked out over an itty-bitty kitty."

"I did not freak out." Kiana glares at him.

"Your scream probably registered on the Richter scale," Kyle jokes.

"You were too scared to even look in the closet." Kiana whirls away from Kyle to point at me, her fear switching to fury. "Kelsey, this is all your fault! Your cat destroyed my homework!"

Uh-oh. Now I have a monster to deal with—my angry sister.

"She's only a kitten and doesn't know any better," I say in a mouse-squeak. Usually Kiana is nice to me, but when she's angry—watch out! Arguing never works. My best strategy is to apologize and beg forgiveness. "I'm really sorry, Kiana. I'll help you rewrite your book report."

"As if a seventh grader could do high school homework." She makes a harrumph sound.

I hug Honey tightly to my chest, not sure which of our hearts is beating faster. "She won't do it again."

"She better not," my dad puts in firmly. "Kittens are too full of energy to run loose in a house—especially a house we're living in rent-free due to the generosity of my new employer. We have to be careful not to damage anything. No stains on the carpet or broken windows or marks on the walls."

I groan. Not another lecture about taking care of our new home. Sure, I'm grateful to Mr. Bragg. (That's King Bragg from the resort hotel commercials with him wearing a crown while sky-diving into a luxurious swimming pool.) But Dad is so afraid something will go wrong and he'll lose another job that he's stressing everyone out. It's not like we're toddlers who draw on walls or spill juice on the carpet. Besides, the only reason King—I mean, Mr. Bragg—offered us this house is because he wanted his new personal chef nearby to prepare his meals 24/7.

"I assured Mr. Bragg that my family was responsible," Dad continues, not noticing that my siblings have sneaked away. "But Kelsey, I can't allow a destructive animal in this house."

"She's not destructive, just playful," I argue as my kitten bats at my hair.

"And very sweet," Mom adds, stroking Honey's

silky fur. "But I agree with your father. Kelsey, you must keep a close watch on your kitten."

"I will," I assure my parents. "Her litter, food, and water are in my room. I'll make sure she doesn't sneak out."

"If she causes any more trouble she has to go," Dad warns.

"No!" I hug my kitten to my chest. "Honey won't do anything wrong again. She'll be a perfect little angel. I promise."

I hope this is a promise I can keep.

Dad offers to make tacos for lunch. His tacos are always delicious with his special seasoning and juicy organic tomatoes. I leave Honey curled in her cushioned cat bed in my room.

"You stay right there and don't get into any trouble." I wag my finger at her.

She blinks her golden eyes innocently, as if to say, "Cause trouble? Me?"

"Yes, you," I say firmly.

I don't know how she got into my sister's room, but I have to make sure she doesn't do it again. I can't lose Honey after waiting so long to bring her home. She was one of three kittens Becca, Leo, and I rescued from a dumpster. At first we secretly cared for them in the Skunk Shack, our CCSC clubhouse, until Leo was allowed to take his kitten home. Then Becca brought her kitten and mine to live in her house. Stuck in an apartment that didn't allow pets, I didn't think I'd ever get to keep Honey and would only be able to visit her after school and on weekends. Then Dad got a job, and it came with a house big enough for my large family, our energetic dog, Handsome, and my sweet kitten. Now every night I fall asleep to Honey's purring lullaby.

I am *not* giving her up.

Shutting my door firmly, I hurry downstairs to join my family around the dining table. I plop a crispy taco on a plate and take a big bite. Spicy tomato juice dribbles down my chin and I lick it off. Yum.

When my brother reaches for his third (or fourth) taco, Dad grins. "As the chef, I take that as a compliment. But don't stuff yourself. We have an important dinner tonight." Dad winks, as if we need reminding despite him telling us a zillion times about our dinner invitation to Bragg Castle.

It's not really a historical castle but it sure looks

formidable with massive stone walls and turrets spiraling to the sky. It's just past a grove of trees beyond our new home. I can't wait to see inside the castle. But I'm kind of nervous too, because King Bragg is famous and I won't know what to say to him. I'm better at listening than talking.

I'll ask Becca for advice. Her CCSC title is Social Contact Operative, and she can talk to anyone. Sometimes I think she can talk to animals too, or at least understand what they're saying since she helps her mom run their animal sanctuary. When I called her earlier, she was getting ready to give a bear a bubble bath. Yeah, a real bear.

Becca and Leo, our club's Covert Technology Strategist, will be here in an hour to see my new home. When Dad first told us we were moving into a cottage, I expected something small and cozy like out of a fairytale. But a five-bedroom house is a cottage to the King of Resorts when compared to his castle. I wonder if there will be suits of armor propped up like guards, secret passages, or a dungeon. Exploring a dungeon would be cool.

After lunch, I head up to my room to check on Honey. The door is shut just like I left it. As I step inside, I say, "Honey, I'm back."

She doesn't romp over to rub my ankles or meow to be picked up. And when I look at her kitty bed, only a catnip toy and fuzzy red blanket are there.

My cat is gone.

- Chapter 3 -
Cat-Napped

Honey has to be in my bedroom somewhere. I look beneath my bed. Nope. I check behind my desk. Nope. The closet is open a crack, but when I search inside, still no cat. Impossible! She couldn't turn a door knob or lift a latched window. Could someone have taken her?

Suspect #1: Kiana. Motive: Revenge for her ruined homework.

Is she trying to get my cat in trouble so I can't keep her?

She is not getting away with it!

I start for my sister's room but as I pass my window I catch a flicker of movement outside and see orange. To be exact, the soft orange shade of Honey.

How did my cat get outside?

I practically fly down the stairs, the front door banging behind me. Honey is crouched in the grass, stalking an unsuspecting leaf. She loves to pounce on leaves like they're birds or mice. It's funny to watch her strut around with a leaf in her mouth, like a trophy she's showing off.

But nothing about my escapee-cat is funny now.

"Bad kitty," I say as I scoop her up in my arms. She mews and her leaf floats to the grass. "How did you get out here?"

She licks my arm and I giggle because it tickles. She's so soft and sweet, and I'm just relieved she's safe. I run my fingers through her orange fur, my anger melting away.

A fanged monster with a spiked tail? I smile. *What was my sister thinking?*

Honey squirms in my arms. I follow her gaze to the enormous tree that towers over the front yard. It's so huge it eclipses the house and it's so dense I can't see through the leafy branches. *A good climbing tree,* I decide. I've had a lot of experience climbing trees, especially on CCSC stakeouts. A shady tree with sturdy branches can be a spy's best friend.

I carry Honey to the porch swing and she settles comfortably on my lap. The swing squeaks as I rock back and forth. I scratch Honey in her favorite spot just below her chin and she purrs loudly. "No more escaping, you little Houdini. You have to be good."

She looks at me with big golden eyes as if to say, "How could I be anything but perfect?" I just laugh.

When I hear a humming motor, I look up and see Leo zooming toward me on the homemade robotic skateboard he calls a gyro-board.

"What are you doing here so early?" I ask as he rolls to a stop, gravel spitting from his wheels.

"Should I leave?" Leo asks with an uneasy frown.

"Of course not." I gesture for him to come up to the porch. "Let's wait here for Becca so I can give you both a tour together. She won't be here for a while."

"Twenty-two minutes, if she's punctual." Leo hops off his gyro-board and flips it up to balance on one end. "To be honest, I came early on purpose."

"Oh?" I raise my brows.

"I thought we could...you and I, or is it you and me?...could talk."

He sounds more awkward than usual. My spy senses flash alert and I study Leo. He looks normal enough in dark slacks and a vest over a white shirt. But he seems nervous, shifting his feet and twisting the gyro-board remote in his hand. He's not meeting my gaze either. He's looking down at my feet as if my sneakers are encoded with a secret message.

"Talk about what?" I ask in an encouraging tone.

"It's nothing…I mean…uh…just a question…" He looks away from me.

"About what?"

"Nothing really…I mean…umm…"

Stammering from precise Leo? Something is definitely up.

"Want to sit down?" Smiling, I pat a spot on the swing.

"Next to you?"

"I don't bite, although Honey might," I tease.

Fair-skinned Leo blushes like his face is on fire. As a collector of secrets, I can tell Leo is working up the courage to confide in me. Does it have to do with his new drone project? Yesterday he hinted that his new project will be both "huge and minuscule"— whatever that means.

As I scoot over to make room for Leo, Honey suddenly leaps off my lap and scurries over to the huge oak. She crouches by the trunk, her gaze sharp like a predator at something gray that disappears into leafy branches. *Probably a squirrel,* I think. And then Honey springs up the tree trunk. In a blink, my kitten is gone—as if the massive tree has swallowed her.

"Honey, come back here!" Jumping off the porch, I run over to the tree and peer up. But I only see leaves.

"Don't worry about her," Leo says, coming beside me. "According to my calculations, a cat will come down from a tree in three to five days."

"I can't wait that long!" I stare anxiously up into dense branches for any sign of my kitten. "I have to get her now or she might get hurt. I think she's chasing a squirrel but I can't see anything except leaves. And the lowest branch is way over my head. How can I get up there?"

"Want a boost?" Leo clasps his hands together and holds them out to me.

"Thanks," I say gratefully.

I lift one foot carefully into Leo's hands. Is he strong enough to hold me? I don't want to break him. But his grip is steady. I gaze up, searching for any sign of my cat. I see a flash of orange and then it's gone. The tree is even bigger than it looked from my bedroom window. It reminds me of Jack's Beanstalk. Branches with dense leaves blot out the light as if there's no sky, only endless tree.

Reaching high, I still can't grab the lowest branch. "Drats. Can I climb onto your shoulders?"

"Wouldn't it be easier to climb on that?"

Jumping back down, I follow Leo's gaze to the far side of the trunk. At first I don't notice anything unusual until I realize an area of bark doesn't match the rest. A worn wooden slat is nailed into the bark, blending in like a shadow. More slats rise up the massive tree trunk.

"A ladder!" I exclaim.

"Incorrect term," Leo says with a critical shake of his head. "A ladder is a structure consisting of a sequence of steps or bars between two upright lengths of wood or metal. These slats are nailed to the tree." He points upward. "If you want your kitten, I suggest you start climbing."

I look up, up, up. How far will I have to go to find my cat? Except for that glimpse of orange, I haven't seen or heard even a mew from her. And it's impossible to see beyond the curtain of leaves. I wonder who put up these slats.

I grab the first slat then use it for balance as I

scoot up higher and reach for the next slat. I pause to peer down at Leo. "After I get Honey, we can finish talking about whatever you wanted to ask me."

"Um...it can wait. Becca will be here soon and it's not something I can say in front of her."

"Why not?" I ask, surprised.

"Um..." He clears his throat. "She would misconstrue the objective of my query."

"Huh?" I grasp the next slat and my leg dangles in the air until I find my footing on the next slat. "Speak English, please."

"Um..." His voice is almost a whisper. "Becca might get the wrong idea...I mean, I know she has a lot of friends...and she probably is...well..." He takes a deep breath then asks quickly, "Does she like anyone?"

"Becca likes everyone! But if you mean like a boyfriend, the answer is no. Although I think Trevor Auslin likes her," I add, chuckling. Leo is 100 percent confident when it comes to book-smarts but socially, he's 100 percent clueless. Becca is the easiest person in the world to talk to, so why is he so nervous?

I'm about to ask him when my hand slips. Rough bark scrapes against my skin as I slide. I dig my fingers like claws into the bark and come to a stop.

"You okay?" Leo calls up.

"Just a little oops." My palms sting but I grab the next slat.

"Can you see your kitten yet?"

"No. I'm getting worried." I reach for another slat, balance, swing my leg up, and grab the next one. Reach, swing, grab, repeat. The slats are evenly spaced up the tree—until they abruptly end at a ceiling of branches.

"Why did you stop?" Leo sounds far away.

"No more slats." I push and tug at the branches over my head. A leaf falls into my hand. Something is odd about the leaf; the green color is too bright and shiny. I press it between my fingers. Plastic! When I look closely at the leaves directly over my head, I discover they're fake too.

What are plastic leaves doing in a living tree? I touch the spot from where the leaf fell and feel a solid surface; not branches or leaves, but a board.

Puzzled, I push at the board until it lifts, revealing a gaping hole. I poke my head through the hole and stare in astonishment.

"Leo!" I shout down. "I've found a tree house!"

- Chapter 4 -

Up in a Tree

"A tree house?" Leo's voice wafts up to my high perch.

I peek through the hole. Inside, there's a metal table with rusty legs; torn cushions that may have fit the small green couch; a crate; a cooler; and three metal folding chairs, one lying on the floor. When I look down to the ground, Leo seems very far away. I hear a whirling sound and push aside a twig to peer up the driveway. Becca is pedaling toward us on her bike.

"Becca's here," I call to Leo. "Tell her what I found, then both of you come up here. I'm going to check out the tree house."

Leo nods and hurries toward Becca. I pull myself

through the hole until I'm inside. It's a mess of dust, dirt, and animal droppings, and it stinks too.

Spotty trails of animal prints crisscross the wood floor and over the top of a filthy table. Dust puffs up around my feet as I cautiously step forward. I stare at the tracks, wondering what animals scampered through here. I'll ask Becca since she knows more about animals than I do. I don't see any animals now—including Honey. Where did my cat go?

A dark shape moves in a shadowed corner. I jump back, my heart pumping fast. On the crate, a stubby tail swishes and golden eyes flash.

"Honey!" I reach out for my kitten. She mews as if to say, "About time you showed up," and springs into my arms.

"I was so worried." I kiss her head. "You're a very bad cat or maybe very smart. Did you lead me here on purpose?"

I'd like to think she's a clever detective kitty but cats just like to chase anything that moves. She saw a squirrel and instinct kicked in so she chased it. Still, if she hadn't climbed the tree, I would never have noticed the slats and found this tree house.

Hugging her, I return my attention to the tree house. There are no windows, only cracks of light coming through loose boards. From the dust and stale air, I doubt any human has been here for a long time. There's evidence of an interrupted lunch. On the table are two red plastic plates, three plastic forks, and two soda cans on their sides. There's a third plate and can underneath the table. While small wild animals probably ate every scrap of leftover food, I doubt they could have toppled over a chair.

Someone left in a big hurry.

Did kids play here? I wonder. Who were they? Did they live in the cottage too? Dad didn't mention who lived here before us. The number of sodas, chairs, and plates show there were at least three kids.

Voices snap me out of my thoughts, and Becca's dark head pokes up through the trapdoor. Honey squirms in my arms so I let her down.

"Coolness!" Becca says as she climbs inside with Leo behind her. Glitter in her leopard-patterned scrunchie shines as her black ponytail sways. "I can't believe this is here. I couldn't see anything from the ground except leaves."

"Plastic leaves hide the tree house like a huge invisibility cloak," I say. "I thought the leaves looked kind of odd but I had no idea they hid a tree house."

Leo sneezes then pulls a white handkerchief from his vest pocket and covers his nose. "It's too dusty in here."

"I like the dust because it shows us clues to the animals that have been here." I point to the floor. "Becca, can you identify the animal prints?"

Becca squats down. "These fresh ones are easy—your kitten. Hmm, I think this is a raccoon paw print and there are more in different sizes like a raccoon family was partying here. The smallest ones could be rats. I'm pretty sure those are squirrel. Those long skinny prints look familiar, like bear prints but too tiny."

"I'll take photos to analyze later," Leo says, his voice muffled through his handkerchief. He takes his phone from his pocket, aims, and clicks.

Becca picks up something from the table between her thumb and finger. "Yuck. A dried banana peel."

I blow dust off one of the soda cans and hear a sloshing sound from inside. "Why leave an unopened soda on the table?"

"Maybe whoever was here was interrupted," Becca says in an ominous tone.

"By a tragedy," I add dramatically. "I can imagine it now—kids hanging out here, getting ready to have lunch. Then something terrible happened… maybe the trapdoor was left open and one of the kids fell…" I shudder at the image.

"Horrible!" Becca steps away from the trapdoor even though it's closed.

"And illogical," Leo scoffs. "If there had been a serious accident, this tree house would have been torn down. The more likely scenario is that the previous inhabitants moved. According to my calculations, considering the accumulation of dust, humans haven't been here in 3.5 months."

"But how did the wild animals get in?" I wonder as I scan the room.

"The same way we did." Becca points at the floor.

I shake my head. "The trapdoor was shut when I found it, and I had to push hard to get it open. And there aren't any windows."

"What's this?" Leo goes over to a large square board on a wall. He shoves with both hands against the board and it splits in half, swinging out to reveal a window.

"Fantastic view!" Becca says, coming beside Leo.

"A camouflaged window." A branch slaps against Leo's arm as he learns through the opening. "I can see across the driveway and woods and even the top of Bragg house, but no one can see us because we blend in with the branches."

"But we still don't know how Honey got inside." I knit my brows together, and sweep my gaze around the room. It's like a locked-door mystery when a crime is discovered in a locked room and the detective must figure out how the bad guy got in and out without anyone knowing. Only there's no crime here—just a curious kitten that chased a squirrel up a tree.

"Where did the squirrel—or whatever creature Honey was following—go?" I wonder aloud. "There has to be another way in and out."

"I don't see any." Becca turns slowly in place, surveying the room.

"Honey was on that crate," I say. "Maybe there's a hole behind it." I walk over and look, but there's nothing. "Not here."

"Maybe under the old couch," Leo says but he doesn't find anything either.

"Honey, if only you could tell us your secrets." I cuddle my kitten in my arms and look into her golden eyes. "How did you get in here?"

Honey meows and squirms.

"I think she understands you." Becca smiles.

"Or she wants to chase the squirrel again," I say with a laugh. On second thought, chasing the squirrel again isn't a bad idea, so I let Honey go. She springs from my arms and pads across the dusty floor, adding a fresh set of prints.

Honey sniffs a dark pile of something gross under the over-turned chairs. She circles around a table leg, her stubby tail swaying behind her. She paws at a shredded cushion then leaps to the couch frame. Not in any hurry, she gazes around like a window shopper.

I cross the room and pat her head. "You're cute but no help."

As I pet Honey, my gaze drifts down to the animal prints overlapping each other in dusty squiggles on the floor. Hmmm. Why so many prints in this corner?

I place Honey on the crate then push aside the cooler.

"Ooh, yuck." I wrinkle my nose as a musty odor wafts up from a disgusting pile of decaying leaves, twigs, and tufts of fur. There are random objects too: a rusty spoon, broken pen, tarnished dime, silver key, and rhinestone beads. But it's what's behind the garbage pile that makes me gasp.

"Leo, Becca—look!" I point to a shadowy hole in the wall. The hole is no bigger than my hand with splintered edges and snagged bits of animal hair.

"So that's how the animals got in and out." Becca leans over.

"It's so dark I can't see the other side," I say.

"Poke your hand through to find out," Leo says with a challenge in his tone.

"Me? No way!" I think of spiders and other creepy-crawlers that could lurk in that tunnellike hole. "At least we know how Honey got inside."

"But we haven't learned anything about the kids who came here," Becca adds with a wistful glance around the room. "I wonder if they were younger or older than us and if I've ever met them."

Leo gestures to the table with its dusty soda-can centerpiece. "We know they liked soda."

"What else did they leave behind?" I turn to the cooler. It's so faded (or just really dusty) that it's more pink than red. Its hard plastic sides are speckled with dirt and animal prints. I push aside a sticky cobweb (relieved not to see the spider that made it) then blow off dust and lift up the lid.

Becca peers over my shoulder and sighs. "Only more snacks and drinks."

I sigh too, because I'd hoped to find something mysterious. Unfortunately real life isn't as thrilling as the plots in my mystery books, where an old clock reveals a hidden will, a brassbound chest hides love letters, or a haunted attic holds dazzling jewels. All we find in the cooler are four orange sodas, more chip bags, a box of chocolate-chip granola bars, and a baggie with shriveled blackish things that might have been carrots.

I start to close the cooler when I notice an edge of blue poking out from beneath one of the soda cans. Pushing the can aside, I slide out a thin plastic pouch. I slide the zipper open and see some papers inside. A thrill pulses through me. Hidden papers in a hidden pouch in a hidden tree house! Could they be pages from a secret journal? Love letters? A treasure map?

"What's inside?" Becca asks, tugging on my arm.

I lift out the papers. The first page is blank except for black-inked letters: *Property of ARC.*

I reach deep inside and pull out a bundle of green paper.

No, not paper: fives, tens, and twenty dollar bills.

Over two hundred dollars!

- Chapter 5 -
Cash and Clues

We stare at the money, our mouths open in surprise.

Why would anyone abandon money in a tree house? I can understand leaving food behind. But money? Especially so much! I don't care how big of a hurry I was in, I'd come back for a pouch of money. Something really terrible must have happened to the kids who hung out here.

Did one of them get sick or even worse?

"Can I count the money?" Leo asks with his palm out.

Nodding, I hand the cash over and watch him quickly shuffle through the bills. "Two hundred and twenty-nine dollars," Leo announces.

"Wow!" Becca exclaims. "That's like a fortune."

"It's more than we've ever had in our CCSC treasury." Leo fans the cash in his hand. "The most was one hundred and four dollars, and that's only because of a one-hundred-dollar reward for returning that Chihuahua with the jeweled collar."

"We didn't have that much for long because we donated half to the Humane Society," Becca adds proudly.

We use half of any money we earn for club expenses then donate the other half to animal charities. Helping animals is our club goal.

I finally ask the question that I know we're all thinking.

"What are we going to do with it?"

We stand there awkwardly, surrounded by dust and cobwebs, looking at each other as if waiting for someone else to come up with the answer.

"It doesn't belong to us so we can't keep it." Leo slips the cash back in the plastic container.

"We have to return it to the kids who hung out here," Becca agrees. "Do you think they go to our school?"

"Maybe," I say. "But then why not come back for their stuff? It's obvious no one has been here in months." I tap my finger on the rim of the cooler, shifting into detective mode and mentally adding up clues. "We know one or more people—probably kids—were getting ready for lunch when something happened."

"They liked to play games," Leo adds as he uses his handkerchief to pick up a dusty deck of cards from beneath a chair.

"If they're still in Sun Flower, we can find them," I say with rising confidence.

Leo looks skeptical. "If they didn't come back for the money, they probably don't want to be found."

"Maybe they witnessed a crime." I shudder. "If they're still alive, they could be in a witness protection program."

"Nothing tragic happened to any kid around here, or I would have heard." Becca reaches up to touch her crescent moon Sparkler necklace. "Rumors buzz around school—like that girl falling off her bike. Everyone was talking about her even before she returned to school with a cast on her leg. But I've never heard any rumors about a tree house tragedy."

"Most likely the kids moved away," I decide, sighing because moving isn't mysterious. I should know—I've moved twice in one year.

Leo's gaze sweeps over the filthy floor and dusty table. "According to the evidence here, there were a minimum of three kids and it's unlikely all of them moved simultaneously."

"Unless they're in the same family," I say. "Like my family."

"Good point." Leo folds his handkerchief then slips it into his vest pocket. "But the question still remains: why leave the money?"

"And how do we find them to return the money?" Becca adds.

"Sounds like a mystery for the CCSC." I get that familiar thrill of excitement and can't wait to pull out my spy pack hidden in my closet. "I'll ask my dad what he knows about the people who used to live in our house."

"I'll analyze the photos when I get home." Leo aims his phone and clicks more pictures.

"And I'll find out if the kids went to our school," Becca offers with a sweet smile that could turn even an enemy into a friend. She knows more people at school and on social media than I'll probably meet in my entire life.

"First let's read these." I hold up the papers I found in the cooler.

"*Property of ARC*," I read aloud. "What does ARC stand for?"

"Isn't it obvious?" Leo says. "The acronym represents a name. For instance, my initials are LNP."

Becca scrunches her forehead. "Leopold *what* Polanski?"

"That's classified information." Leo glances away, avoiding our gazes as he bends down to snap a photo of dried animal poop.

"Classified?" I roll my eyes. "My middle name is old-fashioned but it's no secret. I'm named after my great-grandmother, Alfreda."

"And I have two middle names after my aunts—Laurie Marcella," Becca says. "Leo, tell us yours."

But he shakes his head, his lips pressed tightly like they're glued shut.

"Why won't you tell us?" I persist. "It's just a name."

"A humiliating name."

Now I really have to know. Curiosity itches like a bad case of poison oak and the only cure is finding out the truth.

"You can trust us, Leo," Becca says in her sweetest tone. "We're more than club mates—we're friends."

His face reddens and he shifts his gaze to his dust-speckled black shoes. "I never tell anyone," he says.

"It'll be listed in public records," I point out. "I could look it up."

"A friend would respect my privacy." Leo frowns.

"Well..." The itch to know what N stands for has risen beyond curiosity to a quest. Still, Leo is my friend. I sigh. "All right, I won't research your name. But if I guess right, will you tell me?"

"Yes." Leo smirks. "Because you will *never* guess."

A challenge I can't ignore. "Nathanial, Nickolas, Noel, or Ned?"

Leo shakes his head. "Incorrect."

I try again. "Neil, Norman, Nathan?"

"Not even close. If you knew, you'd tease me."

"Tease you?" I say in mock innocence. "We would never."

"Never," Becca echoes but ruins the sincerity of her promise by giggling.

"It must be really embarrassing." I snap my fingers. "Are you named for the mythical god Neptune?"

Now I'm giggling, which sets off Becca. When

Leo glares at us, I feel guilty for teasing him so I say sorry, then switch the subject by waving the papers in my hand. "Let's see what else is in here."

"A secret code!" I snap my fingers. "I've been studying codes forever."

"It could be a geometry equation." Leo traces his finger across the odd symbols.

"Or doodles," Becca adds. "I love to doodle fashion designs."

"I'm sure it's a code. I can look it up in my *Deciphering Cryptic Codes* book," I offer. "It's in my room. I'll go get it."

"Look it up later," Becca says with a wave of her purple-polished fingers. "What's the next paper say?"

I fold up the first page of codes and tuck it into my pocket. The next paper has two columns of handwritten (messy) names:

Bandit	Dehydration
Muffy	Bloody foot
Willow	Animal bite
Bagel	Infected ear
Skitty	Hypothermia
Xavier	Head trauma

"This list seems strange." Becca knits her dark brows together. "The names are weird too. Who names a kid Bagel?"

"Someone who loves bagels?" I think of Dad's berry-swirl bagels and smack my lips.

"I know!" Becca jumps, and the wood boards beneath our feet quake. "These names aren't for people! They're animals."

"Interesting theory," Leo says with a thoughtful tilt of his head.

Suddenly Becca's expression changes. "OMG! I was worried about one tragedy. But there are six!"

"I know dehydration means lack of water." I turn to Leo. "But what's hypothermia?"

"When your body loses heat faster than it can produce heat," spouts off walking-dictionary Leo, "It causes a dangerously low body temperature."

"Dehydration, a bloody foot, ear infection,

animal bite, head injury, and freezing...maybe... to death." I shiver even though the warm sunlight streams through the cracks in the wood beams over my head.

Becca frowns. "I hope no one died."

"These injuries are painful but rarely lethal." Leo presses his lips together as he stares at the paper. "I'm intrigued by the medical terms. Not many kids know the meaning of hypothermia and can also spell it correctly."

"Why make a list of injuries?" I ask.

I turn to the last page and read out loud.

MEMBERS:
1. RJ
2. GAVIN
3 ZEE ZEE

"Are these human or animal names?" I wonder with a glance at my kitten, who is watching us curiously from her perch on the crate.

"Human," Leo says without doubt.

Why is Leo always so sure he's right? I'm annoyed, but I agree with him this time.

Adding up the clues, we know at least three kids

met here: RJ, Gavin, and Zee Zee. Once we find them, we can return the money.

"There's a girl in my science class named Rachelle Jennifer but everyone calls her RJ," Becca says. "Also, there's a Robert Junior who goes by RJ on the track team. And I have three online friends named Gavin."

"Know anyone named Zee Zee?" I point to the paper.

"No. But it makes me think of Zed. I miss him." Becca glances out the window, as if she can see all the way to Nevada where the zorse she used to care for recently moved. Zed—a hybrid horse/zebra—stayed at Wild Oaks Sanctuary until the Curious Cat Spy Club found his owner.

"So go see him," I urge. "We have a whole week off school. Ask your mom to drive you to Nevada to visit Zed."

"I'd love to. After Mom's hard work at the Humane Society Fund-Raiser, she could use a break." Becca's frown curves into a hopeful smile. "It would be a fun road trip."

I nod and glance over at Leo to see why he's so quiet. He's staring at the table as if the answers to our questions are written in the dust. Suddenly he snaps his fingers and spins around to face us. "That's it!"

"What?" Becca and I ask.

"The purpose of these papers." Leo's blue eyes shine. "They're notes for a club. This is a membership list." He gestures to the paper I'm holding. "I don't know why they wrote about animals—"

"I think I do!" Becca raises her hand like she's first to answer a question in class. "They were caring for injured pets."

"Then ARC isn't someone's initials," I say. "It's a club name."

"Of course!" Leo smacks his palm on his forehead. "The 'C' is for Club."

"A is for animals," Becca adds.

"R could be for Recovery or maybe Rescue— Animal Rescue Club." I grin. "Doesn't it sound freaky familiar? Three kids meeting in a hidden clubhouse with the goal of helping animals, just like us. I wonder if—"

I'm interrupted by a shout outside.

"Drats! It's Dad!" I spring over to the trap door and lift the handle to peer down through the leafy branches. "He's calling for me and headed this way!"

"Why are you whispering?" Leo gives me a

puzzled look. "Shouldn't you let him know you're here?"

"And ruin all the fun of having a hidden tree house?" I shake my head. "I'll wait till he's gone then climb down. I don't want my family to know about this. It'll be our secret hideaway."

I hold my breath when Dad calls my name again. He walks down the bricked path to the driveway and stops to check out Becca's bike.

Becca squeezes my arm. "He knows I'm with you."

"But he doesn't know we're up here." I put my finger to my lips. "Speak without talking."

"Like this?" She mouths. "Can you understand me?"

I nod.

"I hope he doesn't find us."

"Would you two stop not talking?" Leo complains. He's not a fan of lip-reading since he can't do it.

"Shhh!" I whisper with my finger to my mouth.

The trap door is open a crack so we can watch Dad as he looks around the yard and then up into the tree. I know he can't see us because I stood exactly where he is and only saw dense leaves. Still, I grip the trap door so tightly my knuckles ache.

Becca's nervous fingers dig into my arm. Leo watches too, but his expression is relaxed like he's calculated the odds of our being discovered and determined that they are low.

Dad calls my name once more then shrugs and turns away from the tree.

I blow out the breath I'd been holding. "He's going around to the backyard. This is our chance to leave!"

Becca is already lowering herself through the trapdoor. Her foot dangles inches over the slats. She almost has her foot on the top slat when her fingers slip. She falls and—

Leo lunges forward to grab her wrist. He holds her until she finds her footing.

"Great catch," Becca says breathlessly.

"Are you okay?" he asks.

"I am now...thanks to you."

"I didn't do anything special." He's trying to sound casual, but he's blushing. "According to my calculations, a fall from this distance has only a 19 percent chance of fatality."

"But falling would really hurt." Becca smiles at Leo. "You 19 percent saved my life."

Leo glances away, his face bright red like it's on

fire. I think back to our earlier conversation when he said he wanted to ask me something but not in front of Becca. Is it because he wanted to ask about her? A suspicion hits me, but it's too weird to be true. Logical Leo couldn't possibly have a crush on Becca.

Becca climbs down the tree and Leo follows, staying close. I start after them, until I remember Honey. I call her name and glance around the tree house. Where did she go now?

I hear a rustling behind the cooler.

Dust puffs up around my now-filthy sneakers as I move toward the hole in the wall.

I am really, really hoping I don't have to put my hand in that gross hole. The mess piled beside it is bad enough. I don't even want to imagine what's on the other side of the hole.

Still…I can't leave without Honey. So I get down on my knees, holding my breath to avoid the disgusting smells, and peek into the murky-black hole.

Beady eyes shine back at me.

Wild-animal eyes.

Chapter 6

Dinner Rules

With a gasp, I jump away from the hole.

"Kelsey!" Leo's voice comes from behind me, and I whirl around. His blond head pokes up from the trap door. "Are you coming?"

"I-I was looking for Honey and saw a-a—" I point, my hand shaking.

"What?" Leo looks around curiously. "I don't see anything."

"But there was—" I stop because now there's only an empty black hole.

The eyes are gone.

"It was probably just a rat," I say, calmer now and embarrassed I freaked out over a harmless rodent.

"Kelsey!" My father's voice echoes in the distance. We have to get out of here before he discovers the tree house!

Quickly, I follow Leo down the tree. Guess who's waiting for me at the bottom? Honey's whiskers twitch as if to say, "What took you so long?"

I scoop up my kitten and invite my friends inside to see my new home. The word "home" sounds yummy, sweeter than Dad's fudge cream doughnuts. I used to have an empty place inside me, a sadness I guess, after our home was foreclosed and we moved into an apartment that didn't even allow pets. But this home is a new start and I'm proud to give my friends a tour.

"Mr. Bragg calls it a cottage," I explain as I show them the kitchen. It's twice as big as the one we had in our apartment. As good sleuths we stop to investigate the honey-crumble cookies Dad left out for us. We conclude that they are delicious.

I put on an Australian accent like a tour guide I saw on TV. I lead them upstairs to my room, which is kind of messy so I just give them a quick look.

My brother's door is open but his room is empty. It's tidy as usual like a bedroom in a catalog. He got the neat-freak gene in our family.

Next are my sisters' rooms. I hear voices and

music inside, but I don't knock because I'm still annoyed with Kiana because I'm sure she let Honey out of my room. She's the only one with a motive.

I lead my friends downstairs and show them the family room with its sunny yellow walls, a fire place, and a large picture window overlooking the backyard.

Becca stops walking and cups her ear. "I hear a dog whining."

"Handsome wants to play." I point to a golden-furry nose pressed against the sliding glass back door and a battered Frisbee in his mouth.

I step out on the patio to pat my sweet dog. He's too energetic for me to let in. "He loves his new yard. When we brought him home from Gran Nola's, he was so excited, he ran circles and sniffed every weed and bush. This yard is even bigger than my grandmother's."

"He wants to play Frisbee." Becca grins and tosses the Frisbee for him.

I glance back through the glass door into the house and notice Dad sitting on the couch. I tell my friends I'll be right back and go inside to ask him an important question.

My father has a steaming cup of coffee within reach on an end table. He leans back and flips through his favorite culinary magazine *Adventures in Taste*. He glances up. "There you are, Kelsey. I was looking for you a while ago."

"Oh?" I act surprised like I didn't hear him calling me. "What did you want?"

"To give you this," he says as he pulls out a folded paper from his pocket. "Memorize it so you'll be prepared for Mr. Bragg's dinner tonight."

"I have to study to eat dinner?" I ask, not sure whether to be insulted or amused. "Will there be a pop quiz? Will I be graded on my eating skills?"

"This isn't a joke. It's my insurance that nothing will go wrong tonight. Being the personal chef to Mr. Bragg comes with a lot of responsibilities. He's meeting you all for the first time and you kids need to be on your best behavior. Here." He hands me the paper. "Your sisters and brother already have their rules."

BRAGG DINNER RULES

1. Only talk to Mr. Bragg when he speaks to you first.

2. Say please, thank you, and excuse me.

3. If you don't like the food that's served, eat it anyway.

4. Do not spill, spit, drop, break, burp, or fart.

5. Use the proper silverware, and keep your napkin in your lap.

6. No arguing, hitting, or insulting one another.

7. Do not touch anything without permission.

Follow all these rules and you'll be rewarded.

"Rewarded? Like with money?" I ask hopefully.

"Your siblings asked the same thing." Dad grins. "I was thinking more of a special meal or dessert, but if tonight is a success without any embarrassing moments, we can negotiate the reward."

"I like the sound of that," I say, sitting on the couch. "Dad, I've been wondering about our house. Do you know anything about the kids who used to live here?"

"Mr. King never mentioned any kids." He scratches his head. "The cottage has been empty for a while."

"At least three months," I say.

"Yeah, that sounds right." Fortunately, Dad doesn't ask how I know this. He's pressing his lips together as if thinking. "Mr. Bragg's assistant Angel mentioned that the last chef lived here. I found cookbooks in the kitchen with Deidra written inside. When I asked Mr. Bragg about her, all he would say is she was fired. He seemed upset, so I didn't ask again."

Is that why the ARC kids left the tree house so suddenly? I wonder. *Their mother lost her job?*

When I return to the backyard, Becca is flinging the Frisbee into the air. Handsome springs up to catch it in his mouth.

"I can throw higher than that." Leo tries to take the Frisbee from Handsome but my playful dog won't give it up. When Leo gives a big tug, Handsome suddenly lets go and Leo flies backward, landing on his butt.

"Do not laugh," Leo says, brushing grass from his slacks.

"Too late." Becca laughs so hard she doubles over, and I start to laugh too.

We play Frisbee a little longer until we give Handsome a bone and he retreats to his dog house with it. We relax in the metal patio chairs, and I tell my friends about my talk with Dad. "He says the last chef lived here but she was fired."

"Why?" Becca pushes a strand of pink-black hair from her dark eyes.

"Dad didn't know. But she must have done something really bad." I frown. "Maybe she gave Mr. Bragg food poisoning and almost killed him. Dad said Mr. Bragg didn't want to talk about her."

"So Mr. Bragg probably won't tell you either," Becca warns.

"I'm not going to ask about the chef," I say. "Just about her kids."

"Assuming she had any," Leo points out. "Don't jump to conclusions before researching the facts."

"If I can't find out from Mr. Bragg, I'll ask someone else." I drum my fingers on the table. "Dad mentioned an assistant."

"Angelica Hampton-Kensington is his executive assistant," Leo spouts off like his brain is wired to the Internet. "I searched online and found out Angelica and Mr. Bragg's nephew, Irwin, live in the castle. There's a housekeeper too, but I'm not sure where he lives."

"Any mention of a cook?" I ask, curious about who Dad replaced.

"No. But I read a fascinating article on the architecture of Mr. Bragg's house—it was designed after a Scottish castle."

"I call it Bragg Castle, but I won't tell him that," I say. "Of course I'm not even allowed to talk to him unless he talks to me first."

"Why?" Leo asks.

"Dad gave me Dinner Rules."

I read the rules out loud to them. When I get to number four (*Do not spill, spit, drop, break, burp, or fart*) Becca brings her arm to her mouth and makes a farting noise. Leo is so startled he topples back in his chair, almost falling off. Instead of complaining, he starts to laugh.

We're all so different but we've become best friends, I think, smiling to myself. Becca is creative, outgoing, and the kindest person I know; Leo is logical, loyal, and brilliant with robotics; and I'm quiet, watchful, and good at solving puzzles. Sometimes differences pull people apart, but ours bond us together.

I continue reading the Dinner Rules to my friends. I'm on number six when Becca gets a text from her mother. "She wants me to come home to bottle-feed a baby monkey," Becca explains.

"What do you feed a baby monkey?" Leo asks, raising his brows.

"Special monkey formula. Juniper is so tiny, I have to feed her with a syringe." Becca slips her phone back into her pocket. "Never a boring day at the animal sanctuary. I have to go."

Leo and I walk with her around to the front yard. Sunlight shifts to shadows as we pass under the towering oak tree. I look up into the thick green leaves, smiling at my secret knowledge of plastic leaves, a trapdoor, and a hidden tree house. I can't wait to add this new secret to my collection.

As Becca wheels away on her bike, I peer through the branches for a ropy gray tail and beady eyes. What sort of animal was staring at me?

"Kelsey," Leo says, tapping my shoulder.

I give a start and turn to face him. "What?"

"I'm eager to study the photos and debris I collected from the tree house," Leo says. "I'm going home too."

"Wait, Leo. Didn't you want to ask me something?"

"No." He walks over to get his gyro-board from my porch.

"Yes, you did." I dodge around to face him. "Something you didn't want to ask me in front of Becca?"

He looks down at the remote and shakes his head.

"What was it?" I persist.

Leo hops on his board like he's eager to get away. "I don't know what you're talking about."

I watch Leo zoom away, wondering why he just lied.

- Chapter 7 -
Bragg Castle

A disembodied hand beckons to me.

Not a flesh and blood hand but a brass one attached to a heavy door. The curled fingers look so real—like they could reach out and grab me. I think of horror movies where teens creep into a haunted castle even though they know they may never come out alive.

Could Bragg Castle be haunted? I wonder as I stand at the marble entrance of the home of Dad's new employer. It looks even more like a medieval castle up close, with gray stone walls like a fortress, turrets, and a front door large enough to welcome a dragon. All that's missing is a moat with hungry alligators chewing up unwanted guests.

I clasp the brass hand but don't knock yet because I'm waiting for my family. I'm the only one that ran up all twenty-six steps. (Yes, I counted.)

Mom and Dad climb slowly, and when I glance down at them, I can tell Dad is nervous. He doesn't officially start work until tomorrow, so tonight he's a guest instead of the chef.

I was surprised when Dad insisted we drive to Bragg Castle when it's just across the trees from our cottage. Driving the short distance seemed strange, but I have a feeling this is just the beginning of strange events tonight.

When my sisters, brother, and parents finally join me at the top of the staircase, I lift the brass hand and knock. A thud reverberates through the door.

"Wicked sound," Kyle says. It's nice to see him dressed up in black slacks and a buttoned blue shirt instead of sport tees and khakis. "Most houses have doorbells."

"This isn't like most houses—oh!" I jump back when the door abruptly swings open.

I was expecting a proper butler in a formal suit, but a purple-haired woman grins at us. She's wearing jeans and a lacy blue blouse with angel wing designs across each shoulder. She has an earpiece in one ear and wears a gold-chain necklace and gold hoop earrings. She's my height but I can see maturity in her silver-gray eyes that hints she's closer to twenty than thirteen.

"Welcome to the castle!" she chirps in a cute voice that reminds me of a Muppet. "You all look fabulous and I'm so glad to meet you. Of course I already know our brilliant new chef. I'm Mr. Bragg's executive assistant, Angelica Hampton-Kensington, but everyone calls me Angel. Follow me."

She leads the way in a skippy stride, her hoop earrings swinging. Everyone else hurries to follow her but I lag behind, admiring the fancy furniture and landscape paintings. Mr. Bragg is famous for his resort hotels around the world, so the exotic paintings are probably from his travels.

The house glows with crystal lamps and chandeliers, but there are shadowy corners that remind me of castles with dungeons and ghosts. So when I suddenly see a bulky metallic shape against a wall, my first thought is—a suit of armor! But as I get closer, I don't see arms or legs. It looks like a machine made of chrome with mirrors and glass tubes.

"That's a Seeburg Jukebox, circa 1952. It plays up to fifty records and has rotating animation."

I whirl around and see the cheerful caramel-brown eyes of the king himself! Mr. Bragg wears casual black jeans and a short-sleeved yellow shirt. I know he's at least sixty but his face is smooth and there's no gray in his raven-black hair. I shift my feet, always a little shy with adults I don't know well, especially someone so famous.

"Haven't you ever seen a jukebox?" He straightens his bright yellow and black tie. When I look closer, I realize the yellow designs are bananas.

"Um...yeah," is all I can say, my mouth going dry.

"You must be the youngest Case." He turns to caress the silvery chrome jukebox like it's a favorite pet. "The Seeburg is the jewel in my collection. Isn't it a beauty?"

"Uh...well it's not a suit of armor." I slap my hand over my mouth. Did I seriously just say that? What is he going to think of me? I may have just blown my chance to ask him about the tree house kids.

Instead of frowning, he tosses back his head and laughs. "Never had anyone compare a jukebox to armor."

"Your home is like a castle so I expected a suit of armor," I explain. "But your jukebox is really cool."

"There's at least one jukebox in every room," he says proudly. "I also have a suit of armor, but it's in the toy room."

"Toy room?" I perk up. If there are toys, there could be kids—maybe the same ones who met in the tree house.

"Not toys for little kids." He chuckles. "Vintage games for big kids."

"I love all kinds of games." I pause, working up my courage. "I was wondering if I could ask you—"

"Sorry, but the answer is no," he cuts me off with a stern headshake. "Children are *not* allowed in the toy room."

Children! As if I'm a toddler instead of a teenager! I press my lips together tight so I won't say anything rude. I wasn't going to ask to see his vintage—a word that just means old—games anyway. I want to know about the kids who might have lived here.

He turns back toward his jukebox, smoothing his fingers across the chrome. "Tell you what I'll do," he says in an almost apologetic tone. "After dinner

I'll give you and your family a personal tour of my jukebox collection."

"That would be great," I say, relieved he's smiling again.

"So how are you settling into the cottage?" he asks.

"I love it." *Especially the tree house*, I think. *Does he know about it?*

"That's great to hear. It wasn't easy to find a chef willing to move onto my estate. The cottage isn't fancy, but there are ample rooms for a big family."

"It's perfect for us," I say enthusiastically. "Has it been empty long?"

"Too long." A pained look creases his face as he stares at his reflection in the jukebox. Before I can ask him who lived there before us, he abruptly turns away. "We should go to the dining room. You can see the Wurlitzer jukebox there," he adds. "The others are probably wondering where we are."

He moves quickly, and I have to hurry to keep up.

When we enter the dining room, he points out the jukebox, its burgundy wood gleaming under the light from the chandelier. He takes a seat at the head of the formal dinner table, and everyone else sits down too. I'm not quick enough to choose my seat, and instead of sitting close to Mr. Bragg, I'm at the far end of the table beside my sisters.

I look up when Mr. Bragg taps his spoon against his wine glass.

"Welcome, Case family," he booms across the table. "I'm honored to have you here tonight. My poor overworked housekeeper, Sergei, has been doing double duty taking care of the castle plus cooking, so he's overjoyed we have a new chef."

"I've already planned my menu for tomorrow," my father tells his boss, looking tense. I want to tell him not to worry so much. Mr. Bragg is lucky to have such a skillful chef. But it took Dad so long to find a new job that he lost some of his confidence.

"Before we eat, some introductions," Mr. Bragg says. "You've already met my lovely and competent assistant, Angel." Gold bracelets jangle as Angel lifts her hand to wave. "And this is my nephew, Irwin." Mr. Bragg gestures to a lanky guy with tortoise-shell glasses that swallow his face. "Irwin is studying for a master's degree while working for me. As my heir, he'll be running the company one day."

"Not for a very long time," Irwin says in a rush, his glasses slipping down his nose. When he pushes them up, his elbow bumps his water glass and splashes the white table cloth. His awkward blush reminds me of a grown-up Leo.

"And this is my family," Dad introduces us with a proud look. "My wife, Katherine; son, Kyle; daughters, Kiana and Kenya; and our youngest, Kelsey."

"That's a mouthful of K names." Mr. Bragg grins.

"It just kind of happened," Mom admits with a chuckle. "Since Kevin and I both have K names, we named our first child Kyle. When the twins came, we already had three K names in the family, so why not add two more? The whole K name thing was a family tradition by the time Kelsey arrived."

"I've already had the pleasure of meeting Kelsey." Mr. Bragg winks at me like we're conspirators.

Dad's gaze narrows with suspicion at me. But I just smile because I didn't break any of the dinner rules. Mr. Bragg spoke to me first.

Sergei, a stocky, middle-aged man with a swatch of gelled green hair and piercings in his nose, lip, and ears, comes in carrying a tray of salads. He glowers like he's in a bad mood.

When he politely, but still not smiling, offers a choice of salad dressings, I pick raspberry-vinegar.

As he pours it over my salad, I notice small black and gray hairs on his white pants. My clothes often have similar orange hairs from cuddling Honey, and I deduct that he has a cat or dog.

Everyone settles into separate conversations. I stab a cherry tomato with my fork and listen and observe. It's what I do best. But it's hard to even hear my own thoughts over the din of voices so I resort to lip-reading and pick up fragments of conversations.

"...switched my major to hotel management so I can help my uncle," Irwin tells my brother.

"...a gift from my grandmother." Angel touches a gold chain around her neck.

"...on a safari a ferocious rhinoceros suddenly charged and the tour guide ran away," Mr. Bragg says.

"...took some fashion design classes and was invited to compete on the *Design Diva* reality show," Irwin continues.

Dollar signs dance in Kyle's eyes. "Did you win a lot of money?"

Intrigued, I lean forward to hear Irwin's answer. "My uncle needs me so I turned it down. I have bigger things going on in the resort hotel business."

If Becca had the chance to compete on a fashion reality show, she'd jump at it and probably win first place. She's going to study fashion in college. I've never really thought much about what I'll study in college. I wonder if they have spy classes.

Mr. Bragg's voice booms across the table—"knew not to mess with me, and the rhino ran away!"

Mom, Dad, and Angel laugh. But Mr. Bragg is one of those talkers who never stops, even when he's chewing.

I turn to listen to the conversation between my brother and Irwin, something about dorm rooms and SAT scores. It's boring until I notice how Irwin's gaze keeps sliding across the table to Angel with a hopeful expression. Does he like her? If he does, poor guy has zero chance. She doesn't even glance at him, all business while she talks about travel with my parents and King Bragg.

By the time dessert is served (something like pudding with raisins that look like floating eyeballs), I'm fidgeting in my seat. I have to find a way to talk to King Bragg alone so I can ask about the ARC kids. But how can I ask with my family listening? My parents might think the tree house is unsafe and forbid me to go there. Or worse—my sisters will think it's cool and take over, like the bounce house takeover on my tenth birthday.

After Sergei collects the dessert dishes (mostly untouched), Mr. Bragg stands. "This has been a wonderful evening. Thank you so much for coming."

Are we leaving already? But I haven't found out about the tree house kids yet.

When everyone stands to leave, my hopes crumble like the napkin I take off my lap and toss on my chair.

"The evening isn't over yet," Mr. Bragg declares, and my hopes rise again. "I'm giving your family a tour of my castle, including my vintage jukebox collection. We'll start with the wine cellar." He turns to me with a wicked grin. "Some people say it reminds them of a dungeon."

An almost real dungeon!

I can't wait and hurry out the door.

We follow the king like we're his royal procession, winding down halls and stairs until we arrive at an ancient-looking wooden door.

"Angel, the keys please." Mr. Bragg holds out his hand to his assistant.

She reaches into a shoulder bag that seems much too big for such a petite girl. She fishes around for a few moments then holds out a jangling key.

"Angel keeps me organized," King Bragg explains as he fits the key in the lock. "I'm so busy traveling that I forget where I leave things. Last week I couldn't find my eighteen carat gold-plated fountain pen—a gift from Britain's former prime minister. I tore my office apart searching for it, but then Angel came to my rescue and found it right away like she's psychic."

"Not psychic," Angel chuckles. "It rolled under your desk. That's an obvious place to look."

"I don't know what I'd do without you." He pats her fondly on the shoulder then opens the door to the dungeon.

Mr. Bragg plunges us down shadowed steps into a chilly dark cellar, which really does look like a dungeon. But instead of torture devices, floor-to-ceiling racks hold wine bottles, the glass glinting. But my gaze is snared by what lurks beyond the wine racks—a darkened room bolted with steel bars.

"That's where I store my finest wines," King Bragg explains when he follows my gaze. "The best vintages in the country."

I force a smile to hide my disappointment. A dungeon prison with torture racks and chains would have been more exciting.

King Bragg makes a big show of selecting a bottle then offering it to my father. "A thank-you gift to my new chef," he says.

"Thank *you*." Dad looks impressed as he reads the label on the bottle.

When we start back up the stars, King Bragg pauses to check a metal box on the wall. "Go on ahead, I just need to adjust the temperature."

My family follows Angel and Irwin upstairs, but I purposely lag behind.

This is my chance to talk to King Bragg!

I wait for him to adjust some knobs and shut the door on the temperature control panel. When he turns around, he looks surprised to see me.

"Mr. Bragg," I say quickly before I lose my courage, "Um...your wine cellar is really cool. Thanks for showing it to us."

"As cool as a dungeon?" he asks teasingly.

"Well...almost." I smile. "Your house is like a real castle."

"It should be. It was designed after the MacNobaill Castle in Scotland—minus the ghosts of course." He laughs like this is a familiar joke, so I laugh too, although to be honest I wouldn't have minded seeing a ghost. If ghosts are real, they'd make great spies.

I walk with him up the stairs. "I don't think our house has any ghosts either. It's big and bright, with so much room inside and out. The last kids who lived there must have hated to leave."

"No." Mr. Bragg stops abruptly, his smile sinking to a frown.

"You mean they wanted to leave?" I ask, confused.

"What I mean," he says, his tone icy enough to give a skeleton goosebumps, "is that there weren't any kids."

"Oh...it's just that I thought—"

"You thought wrong," he interrupts. "There have never been children living on my property."

- Chapter 8 -
Game of Bones

Mr. Bragg pushes open the door and strides away without another word to me. Lift foot. Jam it into my mouth. Choke.

I'd been so sure RJ, Gavin, and Zee Zee lived in our cottage and that Mr. Bragg would tell me how to find them. But now I'm more confused than ever.

I run to keep up with Mr. Bragg. Keeping up with his mood changes is even harder. He's friendly and talkative one minute then the next minute, he has an expression that slams like a door with a Keep Out sign. As he continues the tour, he looks over my head as if I'm invisible. Why is he suddenly so unfriendly? All I did was ask a question.

"Avoidance is a reaction to guilt," I murmur,

remembering this phrase from my *Criminal Psychology* book. I doubt King Bragg committed a crime, but I suspect he's hiding a secret.

Or he just doesn't like kids.

I hide my hurt feelings by pretending to be interested in a gilded painting of a fountain with creepy gargoyles spitting water. King Bragg moves on to talk with my parents while I'm counting gargoyles; eight gruesome monsters frolicking in spilling water. They'd almost be cute if they weren't so hideous.

I run my finger over the gold frame, thinking about RJ, Zee Zee, and Gavin. If they didn't live in the cottage then why did they hold club meetings in the tree house? Bragg Castle is surrounded by woods where homes are few and far from each other. And the No Trespassing signs keep trespassers out.

How do I find the ARC kids?

Around me everything has gone quiet. Turning away from the gargoyle painting, I realize I'm alone. Oops. The tour continued without me. I make a few wrong turns until I hear voices. Hurrying down a shadowed hall, I find the others.

"...extremely rare 1940 Gabel Kuro," Mr. Bragg is saying, gesturing to a wood-paneled jukebox.

"The last Kuro that went up for auction sold for over $120 thousand dollars."

"No way!" Kyle gasps. "That's a lot for a music box."

"My jukeboxes represent an era of rock & roll and drive-in movies. My collection isn't about music, it's about history and art," King Bragg says, patting the machine.

My sister, Kenya, takes out her phone, ready to snap a photo when Angel steps in front of her. "Please no photos of Mr. Bragg's collection," she says in her cute Muppet voice, which contrasts with her disapproving expression.

"Sorry," she says. Kenya frowns and I can tell she's annoyed. My sister is obsessed with snapping photos to post online.

"Angel is my watch dog, always protecting my interests." Mr. Bragg turns to us with an amused expression. "She's right about my not allowing photos of my collections. While I have a superb security system, secrecy is the best defense against thieves."

Thieves? I think, surprised that anyone would want to steal a hulking music box. I mean, why not just listen to music on a phone?

As we tour the castle, Mr. Bragg lectures about his jukeboxes like we're on a school field trip. He pats each jukebox fondly like it's a beloved member of his family. He's talking about a Rock-Ola jukebox when Angel suddenly interrupts, "Excuse me, Mr. Bragg."

"Yes, Angel?" He arches his thick dark brows.

"You need to take this call." She touches her earpiece then lifts a silver cell phone from her pocket and hands it to her employer. "It's Mr. Rattanak."

Mr. Bragg snaps his shoulders back and his mouth hardens into a formidable line. It's like watching a friendly cat turn into a fierce tiger. "My apologies," he explains to us. "I'm in the middle of contract negotiations for a hotel on a Cambodian island. I'll leave you in my nephew's capable hands. Irwin, will you finish the tour?"

"Of course, Uncle Franklin," Irwin says with an obedient nod that causes his oversized glasses to slip down his nose. He pushes them up and turns to my parents. "Please, follow me."

I glance over at Dad, hoping he'll say we don't need to see any more jukeboxes because I'm not the only one starting to yawn. (Mom hid her yawn by faking a cough.) My sisters have resorted to stealth texting (probably each other) and my brother looks half asleep. But Dad simply smiles and thanks Irwin.

So the tour-that-may-never-end continues. As Irwin talks, I marvel at how much he reminds me of Leo. They both speak with precise words and can rattle off dates and facts like their brains are online. But physically they're nothing alike. Irwin has a beaky nose and is kind of homely—while Leo has a cute smile and nice blue eyes. (Not that I'd tell him that.)

When Irwin announces the tour is over, I almost applaud.

I feel like I've walked a marathon and am ready to go home—until I notice a door with a brass plaque engraved with the words Toy Room.

"What's that room?" I ask Irwin as if I don't already know.

"Mr. Bragg's game collection," Irwin says. "Antique chess sets and rare board games from around the world."

"There's a suit of armor too," I say.

He blinks at me. "How did you know?"

"Mr. Bragg told about his Toy Room." I

flash a hopeful smile. "He knows I'm interested in medieval stuff. I'd really love to see the armor."

"Mr. Bragg has strict rules about who is allowed in the Toy Room." Irwin glances at the door then back to me.

My heart sinks. Is he going to call me a child and say I'm too young to see grown-up toys?

"But since he told you about the Toy Room, he must have planned to show it to you," Irwin adds with a smile. "It's my favorite room in the castle. These collections are very old and valuable so be careful not to touch anything."

"I won't leave a single fingerprint," I promise.

Mom and Dad stay behind to rest their feet and my sisters ditch the tour and wander down the hall with their cell phones.

But my brother eagerly follows Irwin. Kyle loves all games; sports, electronic, and even board games. Monday nights at our house used to be game night and we'd pull out boxes of board games. My siblings always chose Monopoly, Risk, or Scruples. But when it my turn to choose we played my favorite board game Clue.

The round turret room has a high curved ceiling and six huge windows, all but one draped closed with heavy curtains. The open window invites light into the room. Rays of sun shine across the polished wood floor and glint over a dozen glass cases. In one corner of the room are displays of chess sets under glass.

Right away I spot the suit of armor gleaming in another corner. But when I draw closer, I'm surprised the armor is so small. I imagined knights as tall as basketball players, but this knight isn't much taller than me.

Were people short in the Middle Ages?

I reach out to touch the armor then quickly pull back, remembering my promise to Irwin. I hear him across the room explaining antique games to my brother so I join them.

"These are not toys to be played with but pieces of history, and many are centuries old," Irwin lectures in a fond tone as if this is a topic he enjoys. "Since moving in with my uncle, I've gained an appreciation of antique games."

Kyle peers into a case holding a wooden board with two rows of holes. "What game is that?"

"Pallankuzhi, or mancala in southern India," Irwin adds. "The history of ancient games is fascinating. Have you heard of Chinese Checkers?"

Kyle and I nod.

"But you probably don't know that Chinese Checkers has nothing to do with China or checkers, or that Parcheesi and Sorry! evolved from the game of pachisi." He moves on to a smaller case. "This dice game appears in cave paintings and Indian mythology. But my uncle's most treasured collection is showcased in his chess corner." We follow him to the largest glass case. "This white and black Reykjavik chess set is crafted from camel and buffalo bone."

"Real animal bones?" I ask, frowning.

He nods. "The earliest chess pieces were carved of bone, ivory, or wood. Ivory was the preferred material but bone was more economical," he says then launches into a history lesson dating back to the Middle Ages.

The games are interesting but when he spouts off dates and technical terms, my gaze wanders to the open window.

What was that? I wonder, sure I saw something small and gray swoosh across the slanted roof. It was probably a bird, even though I didn't see wings.

Puzzled, I lean on a windowsill to peer down the steep roof. The view is amazing! I can see the cottage roof, treetops, ribbons of roads, a silvery winding river, and a cluster of dark houses like specks on the horizon. I didn't realize there was a neighborhood so close and wonder if that's where the ARC kids live.

I turn away from the window—and *smack!* I bump my knee into a cabinet door. Rubbing my throbbing knee, I glare at the metal door like it purposely attacked me. Why was it hanging open? I lean over to shut it but pause when I notice something glimmering green from the top shelf.

I have to look.

Spy Strategy #2: A spy must always pay attention to her surroundings.

Inside the cabinet is the most beautiful chess set ever. The pieces aren't carved from dead-animal bones, but from dazzling gems. One set is green (maybe emeralds) and the other is red (rubies?). Each piece is smaller than my pinkie, as if they were created for a child. Did this set belong to a princess or prince from centuries ago?

I know a little about chess because Leo tried to teach me once, but he kept beating me in a few moves, and that wasn't fun at all. Still I know each set of pieces has eight pawns, two knights, two bishops, two rooks, one queen, and one king. The king is the most important piece. Not the most powerful though—that would be the queen. And sometimes even a lowly pawn can checkmate a king.

But these pieces don't look anything like Leo's set. The two opposing armies ride elephants, horses, and camels, with pawns in gold uniforms.

"Ready to go, Kelsey?" Irwin calls out.

"In a minute," I say, reluctant to leave the gleaming jewels.

Why is this exquisite chess set hidden in a cupboard? It should be on display beneath a golden spotlight, not banished to a cabinet. Something else about the set bothers me. I'm not sure what—until I count the chess pieces.

Sixteen rubies but only fifteen emeralds.

The green king is missing.

I open the cabinet door wider to see if the king was knocked over or rolled away. There are two shelves in the cupboard. The bottom is stacked with books about antiques and the top shelf holds only the jeweled chess set.

"What are you doing in there?" Irwin snaps from behind me.

I whirl around. Irwin's hands are on his hips, and

his scowl is a strong clue he's annoyed. I consider acting innocent and pretending I wasn't snooping. I should apologize, but that wouldn't answer any of my questions.

So I blurt out, "Where's the green king?"

"That cabinet is off limits," he says. Worry lines crease his forehead.

"The door was open and I bumped into it—which hurt." I point below my dress to the tiny red mark on my leg.

"I'm sorry you were injured," he says in a kinder tone.

"I'm not bleeding, but I'm curious." I point inside the cabinet. "Are those really rubies and emeralds?"

"Mr. Bragg wouldn't display anything less than authentic," Irwin says with an insulted purse of his lips. "The tour is over. Come away from there."

"What happened to the emerald king?" I persist. "Did it break?"

Irwin frowns. "It isn't my place to say…"

"But you know who broke it," I persist.

"It wasn't broken…I mean…it's just…just…" He rubs his forehead like Leo does when he gets anxious. "I'd rather not talk about it."

"That's okay," I say with a shrug. "I'll ask Mr. Bragg."

"NO! Do *not* ever mention the chess piece to him." Irwin shakes his head. "You have no idea what he's been through. You'll only upset him."

"Upset who about what?" Kyle joins us, flipping a wave of hair from his face. He looks suspiciously at Irwin. "Did you just say you broke a chess piece?"

"No! That is *not* what I said." Irwin presses his hand to his head, sighing. "Honestly, I don't know much because it happened months ago, before I came to live here. What I do know is that my uncle pretends it never happened. I shouldn't tell you more, but I will just so you'll understand why you must never mention it to Mr. Bragg."

"I know how to keep a secret," I say with a glance at Kyle, who nods and pretends to zip his lips.

"The emerald king wasn't broken." Irwin slams the cabinet door shut. "Someone stole it."

- Chapter 9 -
Tailing a Tail

By the time I get home, it's too late to call Becca and Leo so I borrow Mom's cell phone and leave texts for them to come over early tomorrow. We had planned to meet at the Skunk Shack at noon, but my news can't wait.

Questions explode in me like firecrackers as I lock my bedroom door. I pull open the hidden drawer at the bottom of my dresser and take out my notebook of secrets. Grabbing a pen off my desk, I write:

Secret 40. Mr. Bragg's emerald king was stolen.

I stare at these words, wondering if Sheriff Fischer investigated this theft. Did he find clues like fingerprints or signs of a break-in? Were there any suspects? The thief must not be very smart to take one chess piece when the complete set must be worth a fortune.

When I asked Irwin these questions, he clammed up like his lips were superglued. He only revealed this much because of the EOS: element of surprise. I doubt he'll tell me any more. So how do I find answers to my questions?

There are four Ws of investigation: Where, When, Why, and Who-Dun-It. I know where and have an idea of when, but nothing else. Was the motive greed or something more personal like revenge? And the biggest question: who has the emerald king now?

It's all very puzzling, but exciting too—another mystery for the CCSC.

That night I dream of emerald and ruby chess pieces battling like the scene in the first Harry Potter book. The angry emerald queen chases me, waving her royal staff. My legs ache from running but I don't seem to be getting anywhere. The Queen draws closer and closer. She overtakes me and reels back with her mighty staff, ready to smash my head. But the emerald king dodges in front of me, taking the blow on his crown and shattering into shards...

I wake up sweating.

I blink in the darkness. My room is silent except for the distant hoots of an owl and the hum insects. I reach for my kitten in her favorite sleeping spot at the foot of my bed…but she's not there. I click on my bedside lamp. The kitty bed is empty too.

I fling my covers aside and search beneath the bed, behind the dresser, and inside the closet—but no kitty. Like yesterday, the door and windows are shut.

Did Honey sneak into my sister's room again? Alarm jolts through me as I remember Dad's warning about my cat, "If she causes any more trouble she has to go."

I tiptoe down the hall and peek into Kiana's room. She's asleep, her soft breathing drifting from her bed. The closet door is wide open and messy with discarded clothes and shoes. No sign of Honey, so at least she isn't causing any trouble. But if she isn't here, where is she? And did she get out on her own or did someone in my family—like Kiana—let her out? I'm tempted to wake Kiana and accuse her, but she'd never admit it.

After a futile search of the house, I grab a jacket and head outside.

I snap on the outside light and step onto the porch. I rub my eyes, sleepy but more worried about my kitten. Honey is so little and the woods behind our house are full of dangerous predators that would enjoy a kitty snack.

"Honey, Honey," I whisper into the shadowy leaves hiding the tree house. When I hear the shivering of leaves overhead, I spot Honey peering down at me from a gnarled branch.

"Come down right now," I say.

She swishes her tail with attitude, and springs up to a higher branch.

"You're a very bad kitty!" I wave my finger at her. "Get back here!"

But she's already disappeared into dense greenness. Of course I know where she's going, and I grit my teeth as I climb the slat ladder. If I'd blocked the hole in the wall yesterday, Honey couldn't sneak into the tree house.

I'm breathing hard, mostly from frustration, when my fingers find the leaf-shrouded trapdoor. I push up and the door lifts a few inches, just enough for me to see into the room. I'm ready to scold Honey when I freeze like a statue and stare at not one animal—but two!

Honey tumbles playfully across the dusty floor with a small gray creature. It has a ropy tail and is furry like a fuzzy scarf.

Of course, I know what it is, but I'm surprised Becca didn't figure it out when we saw the long paw prints. She did say they looked familiar—and they should have! Becca has two ferrets living at her home at Wild Oaks Sanctuary. She nicknamed them the Fur Bros. When my kitten stayed at Becca's house while I was living in a no-pets apartment, Honey enjoyed playing with the furry brothers. But this ferret isn't a pet—it's wild.

Will it hurt Honey? I worry as it tumbles with my small kitten. I'm ready to rush in to the rescue when Honey affectionately licks the ferret's whiskery face. The ferret nuzzles against Honey, like they're two best buddies. Still, that doesn't mean this ferret is tame like Becca's ferrets. It has a wild, rough look to its gray-brown fur and the black markings of a mask across its beady eyes.

I'm trying to be quiet so I don't startle the animals, but the ferret suddenly turns toward me. Its black eyes stare. The ferret whirls away, stirring up a cloud of dust, and disappears like a puff of smoke.

I'm sure it escaped through the hole in the wall, so I scramble down the tree trunk, the trapdoor banging shut over my head. I stare up into the dense branches, and there it is! A streak of gray skitters down a sloped branch then it seems to fly through the air, landing on the grassy ground.

I know Honey will be safe in the tree house, so I take off after the ferret, curious to see where it's going.

As dawn lightens the sky into pinkish-gold, I can see the ground I'm running on. I swerve around a prickly dark-green bush and keep running through high grasses. The small animal is moving away from our house into the dense pines separating the cottage and Bragg Castle. I keep my sight on its ropy tail and run faster.

The ferret whisks up a pine tree. I lose sight of it until it scurries down the next tree and disappears into the wild grass. The clever little guy is trying to elude me. But I don't give up easily, even though the chilly air is seeping through my jacket and gives me goose bumps up my arms.

Still I continue to follow, my eyes on the waving gray tail. We're almost past the trees where a grassy meadow sweeps up to a wrought-iron fence surrounding Bragg Castle. The fence rises to pointy spires and keeps out all trespassers more securely than a medieval moat. I can't see any sign of movement in the grass until the ferret jumps onto a rock. I pick up my pace and continue the chase. The ferret weaves like a gray ribbon through the grass then slips through the locked gate.

Drats! How can I follow him now?

I don't want to catch him because I don't want to get scratched or bitten. I just want to find out where he's going.

Does he have a home or does he live in the tree house? I wish Becca were here. She'd know how to help him. Her ferrets are very sweet and friendly and come eagerly when they're called. But this guy is running scared.

When I reach the gate, I clasp my fingers around the cold iron bars and scan the yard beyond the fence. I'm at the back of the castle, not the front entrance where the modern paved driveway winds up to the steep stone entry steps. I feel a sense of having gone back in time here, with the wild grasses and shadowy trees and birds chirping morning greetings.

The cunning ferret knew where to slip through

the fence. Unfortunately I can't climb over the iron spikes without becoming a human shish kebab.

Sighing, I turn to head back to the tree house and wait for Becca and Leo. But I stop when I hear a whistle.

It's not the mechanical squeal like a soccer coach blowing a whistle during a game, but a shrill whistling from someone's lips. It's coming from farther along the fence, where I glimpse the tiled roof and chimney of a small building. I peer through the fence at the stone house with its yard framed by an ivy hedge and a cobbled path leading up to the wooden door where a man with green hair stands on the front porch.

Sergei? I think, surprised. So the housekeeper doesn't live in the castle but in his own house. It's half the size of our cottage.

A yellow porch light shines on Sergei's many piercings. Carrying a plastic bucket, he climbs down the porch to the yard. He reaches into the bucket and pulls out a small dish that he sets on the ground. He reaches in again and pulls out another dish, setting it down a little farther away. He does this three more times and then he steps back to the porch, gives a sharp long whistle, and waits.

Waits for what? I wonder.

I hear hisses and rustling, then the grass shivers, and I can see pointy ears, swishing tails, and then lithe animals scurrying to the dishes.

Cats—over a dozen of them!

White, calico, tabby, Siamese, gray, orange, and a scrawny black cat with only patches of fur like he's survived a fire. The cats don't greet Sergei but keep their distance, their bodies taunt and on guard like wild creatures.

But one of them isn't a cat, and my mouth drops open as I stare at the black-masked face.

I've found the ferret.

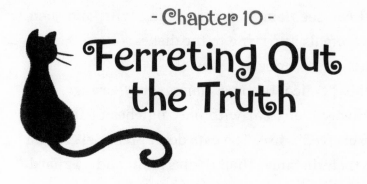

- Chapter 10 -
Ferreting Out the Truth

Before I can call out to Sergei, he goes into the house, and I hear a bolt being latched across his door.

Unable to unlock the gate or climb the fence, I peer through the iron bars at hungry cats crowding around the scattered dishes. A scruffy tabby swats a gray cat away from a dish. The gray cat goes over to a different dish, shoving other cats aside. The cats hiss and swat but mostly they share as if this is a familiar routine.

Do the cats and ferret belong to Sergei?

I doubt it because they crouch around the dishes as if wary of predators. They'd mew to be picked up or petted if they were pets. But these animals are clearly here for the food, a ragamuffin swarm of scruffy fur and feral attitudes. Even their ears are ragged, probably from cat fights.

When I look for the ferret again, I can't find it.

I gaze through the sea of felines for a masked face, but she's gone.

Disappointed, I puzzle over the small ferret and crowd of cats. Why is Sergei feeding them? Is this something he does every morning? I know nothing about Sergei except he's unfriendly and a better housekeeper than cook. I want to ask him about the ferret, but even though I could come back later with my key-spider (Leo's invention) and pick the gate's lock, I'm afraid to face Sergei alone.

So I retrace my steps through the grove of trees back to the tree house. When I climb through the trapdoor, Honey scampers over, swishing her tail with an annoyed attitude. She meows and narrows her golden eyes as if to complain, "Why did you scare my friend away? We were having fun."

"No more fun for you," I say firmly.

Before Honey gets any ideas about looking for her ferret buddy, I scoop her up in my arms. Then I go into my house with a purpose, because there's something I want to do before my friends arrive.

A short while later, I'm wearing my grubbiest clothes and armed with cleaning supplies. Honey trails after me into the tree house.

Since Mom has warned us kids about the dangers of diseases from wild animal scat (a fancy word for poop), I put on plastic gloves and a face mask (borrowed from Mom's animal control truck).

Honey watches from atop the old crate as I pick up the broom. I sweep and fill a garbage bag of leaves, twigs, bits of paper, dried poop, and other yucky stuff. Dust puffs in clouds and makes my eyes water. I consider boarding up the hole in the wall but decide not to because I want to see the ferret again. I think about its silvery-gray markings and dark mask across its face like a bandit.

Bandit! I realize with a start. Wasn't that name listed on the ARC papers? Quickly I open the cooler and unzip the plastic pouch with the papers.

Yes! It's right on the top of the page listing animals and their ailments. Bandit was dehydrated. Obviously he recovered, but why is he living in a tree house and dining with feral cats? Did the ARC kids abandon him like they abandoned the tree house?

I have more questions than answers, and the best way to sort through my thoughts is to do physical work. As I scrub the metal table to a shine, I think about the ferret. I'm sure his name is Bandit. The ARC kids found him and nursed him back to health—but then what? If they cared enough to heal injured pets, why leave the ferret to survive on its own? Or does it belong to Sergei? If so, why is he wandering on his own?

A black stain won't come out of one of the couch cushions no matter how hard I scrub. So I flip the cushion over.

I've saved the worst for last—the filthy pile beside the hole in the wall. It's like someone piled up junk: broken silverware, bits of plastic, clothes scraps, and a headless Barbie doll. Even through my face mask, the musty odor stinks. I push the cooler out of the way and a creaking sound startles me.

I whirl around to see the trapdoor lifting...

"Becca!" I drop the broom.

"Hey, Kelsey!" She flips a tendril of black hair from her face.

"You shouldn't sneak up on me." My words are muffled, so I take off my protective mask and set it on the now-clean table.

"You texted to come early so here I am. But seriously, you need your own phone," Becca complains as she crawls into the room. She straightens up. She's taller than me so her head is only inches from the wood ceiling. "I started to reply to your text until I realized you'd borrowed your mother's phone and—wow!" She interrupts herself to look around, eyes widening. "This room looks amazing!"

"Thanks," I say, pleased.

Becca wipes her finger across the table. "Everything is so clean."

"I still have more to do."

"I'll help while you tell me every detail about last night." Becca reaches for a dust rag. "What's it like having dinner in a castle?"

"Fantabulous," I say using one of my favorite words. I wring out my wash cloth into the soapy water pail. "The castle has lots of cool stuff— including a dungeon!"

She grins. "Any prisoners?"

"Just wine bottles. Oh, and there's a barred room like a prison. And in a turret at the top of the castle there's a toy room with a real suit of armor!"

"Any ghosts?" she asks eagerly.

"No, but there's a mystery," I say with a secretive smile. "I'll tell you more when Leo gets here."

"I'm so curious I could chew my nails off. And that would be a shame since I just had them polished." She puts aside the broom to show me her shining purple and silver fingernails. "At least it won't be a long wait. Leo texted a while ago to say he was on his way."

"Good." I toss the dirty cloth into the bucket. "I have a lot to share."

"I found out something too." Becca's dark eyes shine. "Remember those skinny animal prints we didn't recognize? I'm embarrassed I didn't figure it out sooner. The animal is a—"

"Ferret," I interrupt.

Her mouth drops open. "You already know?"

"I caught Honey playing with a ferret." I gesture to my cat curled asleep on the crate. "The ferret must have shown her how to get in and out of the house."

"Ferrets can slip through openings as small as a few inches," Becca says.

"I also think this ferret is the animal called Bandit from the list we found." I gesture to the cooler. "There's a black mask across its eyes like a bandit.

Oh! I just realized something else—the ferret must have been playing with my cat in my sister's room. Kiana saw their combined shadow and screamed because she thought it was a monster."

"Nothing monstrous about ferrets," Becca says fondly. "When Honey lived with me, she loved playing with the Fur Bros. Cats and ferrets get along great. I should have recognized the paw prints right away." She gives me a sheepish smile. "But I thought it was a wild animal. Ferrets depend on humans to care for them and can't usually survive in the wild."

"He may not be wild," I say. "I saw Sergei feeding him with a bunch of cats."

"Sir who?"

"Not 'sir.' That's his name." I repeat it with emphasis on the two syllables. "Sergei is Mr. Bragg's housekeeper and he has green hair and wicked piercings. He made a yucky dessert that looks like eyeballs floating in Jell-O."

"Eyeballs?" Becca giggles.

"Soggy raisins," I admit. "Sergei never smiled or talked while he served dinner and I thought he was a big sourpuss. But when I followed the ferret to Sergei's house, he was feeding a lot of cats."

"Anyone who's kind to animals is okay with me." Becca's dark brows arch with interest. "Tell me about these cats."

"There were all colors—orange, black, gray, white—and scrawny with rough fur. Even though Sergei was feeding them, they didn't get near him." I bend over to lift Honey of the cabinet and cuddle her in my arms. I stroke her silky fur and she purrs.

Becca strums her fingers on the tabletop. "Did you notice anything unusual about their ears?"

"Yeah," I say as I sit back down. "They were ragged like they'd been in lots of cat fights."

"Or notched for the feral cat spaying program," Becca says.

"Notched? What's that?"

"In some areas, free-roaming cats are a huge problem. So they're trapped and brought into spay-neuter clinics where veterinarians donate their time to cut down on the cat population. Each cat gets a notch in one ear, identifying them as being spayed or neutered. Then they're returned and released."

"Cats can survive on their own but not a ferret," Becca adds with a worried frown. "Bandit needs a home where he's safe from predators and harsh weather."

"I think Bandit lives here and gets in and out through there." I point to the hole in the wall just beyond the huge pile of filth I still need to clean up. I grab the broom and—

"Don't sweep that!" Becca snatches the broom from my hands.

"You want to do it? But your pretty jacket will get dirty." I'm puzzled because she's wearing her favorite pair of black jeans and a tiger-striped jacket over a silky yellow blouse.

"We're not going to clean it because it's a nest. Bandit must be a female ferret," Becca explains, bending over for a closer look. "Females have a nesting instinct and collect items to line their den." She points to a ripped sock sticking out from the bottom of the pile. "If this is Bandit's home, it would be rude to sweep up her nest."

"Can I spray it with air freshener?" I pucker my nose.

"No. Smells are important to animals. We need to let Bandit come and go as she pleases until we can find her a safe home."

"She might belong to Sergei," I say.

"Then why did she make a nest here?" Becca shakes her head.

"I don't know. And Sergei is too scary to question."

"A spy must be fearless when interrogating a subject," Becca quotes.

"No fair using my own quotes against me," I say, but I'm grinning because it's nice to have a friend who knows me so well. "I'll try to talk to him. But I don't know when I'll get a chance. It's not like I'm invited to the castle every day."

"You'll figure out a way. And if you find out that Bandit is homeless then I'll tell Mom and she'll know how to help. I read up on ferrets when we got the Fur Bros. Ferrets lost their hunting instinct centuries ago. They're cute little guys but totally reliant on humans. Bandit wouldn't have survived more than a few days if someone wasn't feeding her. Oh!" Becca cups her hand to her ear. "I hear Leo's gyro-board."

Sure enough, Leo pops up through the trapdoor a few moments later.

"Impressive!" he says as he surveys the tree house. "I can breathe without covering my mouth or sneezing."

"Kelsey did all the work." Becca gestures toward me.

Leo smiles at me. "Great job. You're very efficient."

It feels nice—but strange—to get a compliment from Leo. When I realize I'm blushing, I change the subject. "Nigel?"

"Huh?" Leo blinks.

"Your middle name. You said if I guessed right you'd tell me."

"You're far from guessing right," Leo says with a laugh.

"Nesbitt, Neville, Nyles, Nunzio?"

"Wrong, wrong, wrong, wrong." Smiling smugly, Leo sits in a metal chair beside me.

Sighing, I give up the name game for now and get down to club business. "Now that we're all together, I can tell you about last night. Not only did I get a tour of the castle but I found a mystery to solve."

"Another one?" Leo furrows his forehead. "Our top priority is to return the $229 to the ARC kids— and I've uncovered pertinent information."

"If you're going to tell us the long skinny paw prints were a ferret, we already know," Becca interrupts.

"A ferret?" Leo cocks his head to the side. "That

explains why I didn't find a match online—I was searching for wild animals not domesticated ones. I printed a poster of wild paw prints native to northern California." He pulls out a sheet of paper from his backpack and unrolls it flat.

"Oh, it's lovely!" Becca holds the paper up to catch light. "The drawings are so realistic."

"I have no use for it." Leo offers her the poster. "Keep it."

"Really? Thanks! I'll put it on my ceiling with my other favorite posters." Becca has an "upside-down" bedroom with her belongings high above the floor so they're safe from her goat and other pets.

"It's just a print-out," Leo says with a shrug. "Nothing special."

"But it's special to me. Thanks so much!" She gives Leo a quick hug.

"Um...you're welcome." Leo face burns crimson but he's smiling like he was the one given a gift; not the other way around. And that weird idea I'd had yesterday returns. Could Leo *like* Becca?

Impossible, I assure myself. Leo is too logical for a romantic crush. He blushed because Becca's hug embarrassed him. Besides, they don't have much in common. Leo's an introvert and interested in science—which is more like me than Becca. And Becca already likes someone—Trevor Auslin. If Leo liked her romantically it would be a one-way trip to heartbreak.

"Returning to CCSC business." Leo straightens his shoulders as if to shake off his awkwardness. "Before we take on a new mystery, we need to return the $229 dollars."

"But we don't know how to find RJ, Zee Zee, or Gavin," I point out.

"Au contraire," Leo says in a bad French accent. "I've uncovered new information."

"What?" Becca and I both ask, leaning forward eagerly.

"According to my calculations, the ARC kids age range is ten through eighteen, with a 57 percent likelihood they attend Helen Corning Middle School or Sun Flower High. Without their full names, though, finding them was a challenge. Until I searched Sun Flower High yearbooks"—he pauses dramatically—"and located one of the kids."

Chapter 11

Surveillance

"Her name is Zenobia Zoller," Leo says.

"But her friends call her Zee Zee," Becca guesses with an excited jump.

"Precisely." Leo nods. "She's in ninth grade at Sun Flower High, and I know her address. Let's go talk to her now."

"Wait, Leo!" I cry when he lifts the trapdoor. "It's too early to visit someone we don't even know," I explain. "Zenobia is probably still asleep."

"Who sleeps past 9 a.m. on a weekend?" Leo looks so puzzled that Becca and I giggle. Leo has a habit of assuming others behave like he does.

"I wouldn't have minded sleeping in, but I got here early to hear Kelsey's news," Becca says. She turns to me curiously. "What happened last night?"

"I had a tour of Bragg Castle and found out about a theft," I say in a rush of excitement. "Someone stole an emerald chess piece."

"A genuine emerald?" Leo drops the trapdoor with a soft thud.

"Nothing but the best for King Bragg," I paraphrase Irwin's words from last night with a grin. Now that I have their attention, I launch into the details of my evening with the King of Resorts, starting with the brass door knocker.

"The dungeon was kind of creepy," I say with a delicious shiver. "I loved it."

"Obviously not a real dungeon," Leo scoffs. "American castles can't compare with the historical architecture of European castles."

"Mr. Bragg said his castle was designed after a Scottish castle. The dungeon has thousands of wine bottles and a room with bars like a prison."

"A wine vault," Leo guesses, and I don't bother to tell him he's right.

Instead, I explain how I tried to talk to Mr. Bragg. "It didn't go well." My shoulders slump. "He got mad when I asked about the kids who lived in our cottage. He insists no kids ever lived here."

Becca purses her lips. "But that can't be true."

"This tree house wasn't made for adults," Leo agrees. "The ceiling isn't very high and the trapdoor isn't wide enough."

"Also the club notebook and money we found prove kids were here." I drum my fingers on the table. "Either Mr. Bragg doesn't know about this tree house or he lied to me. But why would he lie? And why did my question make him angry? His nephew, Irwin, acted secretive too, though he's much nicer. Leo, you'd get along great with him." I grin mischievously. "Irwin reminds me of you."

"Do we share a physical countenance?" Leo smooths back his blond hair. "Or are you speaking metaphorically?"

I roll my eyes. "I just meant that Irwin is smart and talks with big words like he swallowed a dictionary. When Mr. Bragg left to take a business call, Irwin took us into the toy room—where I bumped into a cabinet and found a jeweled chess set. The rubies and emeralds were dazzling! But when I counted them I realized one was missing— the emerald king. Irwin told me it was stolen."

"Does he know who stole it?" Becca asks.

"I don't think so. He acted nervous like he regretted

telling me that much and he said not to mention it to King Bragg because it would upset him."

"I'd be upset too if I lost an expensive chess piece." Leo gazes at a stain on the table, his expression faraway like his thoughts are in a distant galaxy, then he blinks and returns to Earth. "According to my calculations, the chess set should be worth eighty-eight thousand dollars."

Becca's jaw drops. "That's a lot for a game!"

"Chess is more than a game. It's about strategy and war and history." Leo strokes his chin thoughtfully. "But why would a thief steal only one piece?"

"Exactly what I wondered," I say.

"Since the chess set is so valuable, there might be a reward for the emerald king's return." Becca's dark eyes shine. "If we can find out who stole the missing piece and there is a reward, we could donate to the feral cat program."

"Only you could turn a mystery into an opportunity to help animals," I say fondly. Becca has a heart big enough to care for every animal in the world.

"We can investigate the emerald king *after* we talk to Zenobia. I vote that we go to her home now. Do I hear a second?"

Becca and I share a look. I have a bad feeling about going on surveillance with little information about the subject, but when Leo gets stubborn there's nothing to do except what he wants.

"Sure," Becca tells Leo, but he just stares at her like he's not satisfied with her answer until she adds, "I second the motion."

"Motion passed." The trapdoor creaks as Leo pulls it open. "The house isn't far from here."

When he describes the route to Zenobia's house, I realize she lives in the neighborhood I saw while peering through the toy room window at Bragg Castle. All the houses looked as small as dollhouses.

"I have to lock Honey in my bedroom before I go," I say as I hold my kitten tight and hurry toward the house. "I just hope she stays there this time."

As I cut through the kitchen, I'm relieved that it's empty. Usually Dad is making breakfast but he left early for his first day of work at the castle. And Mom loves to sleep in on her days off.

I shut Honey in my room (and tell her very firmly to stay here) then go over to my closet and stand on my tiptoes to reach up to a high shelf for my spy pack.

The pack always feels heavy on my shoulders,

and I consider taking a few things out, like the night vision goggles or my fingerprint kit. But I don't want to leave anything useful behind.

Spy Strategy 5: Always prepare for the unexpected.

As I leave my room, I hear voices across the hall. My sisters are awake—and arguing in Kenya's room.

"Give them back!" Kiana shouts.

"I told you I don't have your stupid shoes!" Kenya shrieks.

"You didn't even ask permission."

"Don't blame me—you lost them."

I don't hear the rest because I'm hurrying down the hall, afraid if my sisters see me they'll accuse me of stealing their shoes—which would just be silly because my feet are smaller than theirs.

I leave a note on the fridge for Mom, saying I'm with my friends. Then I join Becca and Leo outside, hop on my bike—and we're off!

It's a short ride to the neighborhood, which feels newer with sprawling homes in pale colors of beige, tan, and ivory, and yards so green and perfect they're probably manicured by the same gardening service.

Zenobia's tawny-brown paneled house is angled

on a huge corner lot. A blue sedan is parked in the driveway, but the house looks dark with closed windows like sleeping eyes. We ride around the block slowly, not wanting to draw attention to ourselves.

After our third time around, Leo slows his gyroboard to a stop in front of Zenobia's house. With no shadowy trees, our only cover is a pick-up truck parked on the street. We crouch low beside the large tires and strategize.

"Either no one is home or they're sleeping in," Becca whispers.

"We can't stand around without a good reason or neighbors will get suspicious," I say with an uneasy glance at the house next to Zenobia's where a cat is meowing at the front door. "Surveillance means watching without being noticed. I'll pretend something's wrong with my bike chain."

"Good idea," Leo approves.

"And I'll check online to see if I can find out more about Zenobia," Becca offers, withdrawing her sparkly pink cell phone from her pocket. "Anyone watching will think I'm calling for help to fix Kelsey's bike." She taps her screen. "Luckily Zenobia is an unusual name...Ah! Found her Facebook page. But only one photo and it's of a bearded rabbit.

Seriously? Doesn't she know anything about maintaining a social media presence?"

"Cute bunny," Leo says as he glances down at the screen.

I tilt my head up from my bike-in-fake-distress position so I can look too. Hands with blue and red nail polish hold the long-haired black-and-white bunny. There's a short caption: *My sweet Muffy.*

"Muffy?" I test the name in my memory. "Why is that name familiar?"

"It's from that animal list in the ARC papers," Leo says. "Muffy had a bloody foot. Bandit was dehydrated. Willow was bitten by an animal. Bagel's ear was infected. Skitty had hypothermia, and Xavier had head trauma."

"You remember all that?" I ask, impressed.

Leo nods like having a photographic memory is no big deal.

"I'm glad Zenobia kept the rabbit." Becca slips her phone back into her jeans pocket. "I wonder what happened to the other animals."

"Zenobia will tell us after we return the money," Leo says confidently, patting his pocket where he tucked the cash.

"I don't think she's home." I straighten up to

look at the house then turn to Leo. "If you had your Dragon Drone or Bird Drone, we could spy through the windows."

"My drones aren't equipped with infrared vision, so they couldn't see into a darkened dwelling."

"What about your new project?" I ask. "Would it work for surveillance?"

"Yes...but it's still in the experimental stage." He reaches into his pocket and pulls out several small objects like popcorn kernels. They're sticky-looking like Scotch tape and reflect Leo's fingers like a mirror without any color of their own. "These are prototypes for my GPF."

"What's that stand for?" Becca asks.

"I'd rather not say until they're perfected." He puts the GPF back in his pocket then asks to use my compact binoculars.

I slip the pack from my shoulder then sift through my spy tools until I find the binoculars.

As Leo peers through them, I watch him curiously, wondering if he's a mystery that needs to be solved too. He's being unusually secretive about his new invention. Also, he's been acting weird, wanting to ask me a question but not in front of Becca, then later denying the whole thing.

And when Becca hugged him, he almost fell over with embarrassment but he had this goofy smile on his face.

I don't want to believe it, but the evidence adds up. Leo has a crush on Becca—which will lead to heartbreak and could destroy the CCSC.

"Kelsey, Becca! Look!" Leo lowers the binoculars and points. "Someone's coming out of the house next to Zenobia's."

I lean forward, squinting at a woman wearing jogging clothes and holding the leash of a large Doberman. She pauses in her front yard to stretch her legs then jogs down the sidewalk—right toward us!

Leo tosses me the binoculars and hops onto his gyro-board. "We have to get out of here. She's headed our way."

I shove the binoculars inside my spy pack but I don't climb onto my bike.

Spy Strategy 11: Knowing when to fight or flee is the mark of a clever spy.

"I think we should stay," I say. "I'll keep pretending something is wrong with my bike, and we're trying to fix it. She won't even notice us."

"And if she does, I'll question her," Becca says.

"This could be our opportunity to find out about Zenobia."

"Or get attacked by a Doberman." Leo frowns at the approaching dog.

"Dobermans get a bad rap. I can tell this one is a sweetie," Becca assures him, boldly walking toward the jogger and her dog.

"We better go with her," I whisper to Leo though I'm uneasy too. I love dogs, but I respect them enough to know to approach a strange dog with caution.

Becca waves at the jogger with one hand and holds out her other hand so the dog can smell her friendly vibes. The dog wags its short tail as it yanks on the leash. When it licks her hand, I exhale the breath I'd been holding.

"Beautiful dog," Becca says. "May I pet him?"

"Bradley loves attention," the woman says, pausing but still jogging in place. Her eyes are hidden behind sunglasses but I can see her face is tan like she's outdoors a lot. She's around thirty and wears an electronic pedometer on her wrist.

"I'm Becca," she says quickly with her widest smile. "And these are my friends, Kelsey and Leo. We were coming to visit Zee Zee but it doesn't look like anyone is home."

The woman's eyebrows arch. "Didn't she tell you?"

Becca frowns. "What?"

"The whole family went on a Mexican cruise for spring break. I'm caring for their pets and plants while they're gone."

"When will they be back?" Becca asks.

"Saturday." She sighs wistfully. "Seven days at sea without the demands of phone calls or the Internet. I envy them."

"My timing sucks." Becca's pink-streaked black ponytail hangs as her shoulders slump. "I've been away and haven't talked to Zee Zee in forever. I don't even know if she's going out with Gavin or RJ."

"I've never heard of RJ, but Gavin is a sweetheart. Such a hard-working boy. He helps out when I need someone to walk Bradley." She stops jogging to pet her dog. "Bradley absolutely loves Gavin."

"Most animals do," Becca says as if she actually knows Gavin. "I thought he and Zee Zee were perfect together."

"They were until…well she'll tell you all about it."

"Did something happen to Gavin?" Becca's hands fly to her face. "Is he ill or was there an accident?"

"He's fine. But his mother…" Sadness pales

the woman's face. "I didn't know her well but she always waved when I jogged past her house. I had no idea…but then no one did until the police showed up."

"What happened?" Becca asks in a gasp.

"Gavin's mother was arrested."

- Chapter 12 -
Doggy Dilemma

When the woman tilts up her sunglasses, her eyes are filled with sadness. "Poor Gavin took it so hard. I saw him the next day and asked if there was anything I could do to help. He wouldn't even talk to me."

"Maybe his mother is innocent," I speak up, scenarios spinning in my head. Had she been framed by a jealous coworker? Did she confess to a crime to protect a loved one? Or did she have a doppelgänger that looked so much like her even her family was fooled? These things happen often in the books I read.

But the jogger is frowning. "She confessed to embezzling money from her employer. She'd been stealing for years and her family had no idea. Gavin was so ashamed, he broke up with Zee Zee, and a few weeks later the house was empty." She points to a rust-brown house farther down the street with a For Rent sign on the lawn. "I'm sure Zee Zee will tell you all about it when she comes back from her cruise. I have to run."

Before we can ask where Gavin moved to, the sunglasses fall back in place. Sneakers and paws pound on the sidewalk as the woman and her Doberman disappear around the corner.

Becca, Leo, and I are quiet as we walk back to the bikes and gyro-board. I climb on my bike and wonder how I'd feel if my mother was sent to prison. It's hard to imagine because Mom is so law-abiding that when she was pulled over for speeding she said, "You're right, officer. I'm guilty and deserve a ticket." I glance at my friends riding ahead of me. Are they thinking about their mothers too? Sometimes Becca complains that her mother is too bossy; Leo resents when his mother treats him like a little kid; and my mother gets so busy she doesn't have much time for me. But at least we have mothers around to complain about... unlike Gavin.

Why did Gavin's mother risk her family and freedom for money? I wonder.

When we near the Bragg Estate, Leo rolls beside me and says he's going home. "I planned to skip my usual Sunday with Dad, but I've changed my mind. I'd like to see him."

"And Mom could use my help with the baby monkey," Becca adds.

So I ride on alone to the electronic security gate at the entrance to the Bragg Estate. I tap in the code then coast my bike down the driveway. As I reach our cottage I glimpse Mom through a window.

After parking my bike in the garage, I hurry into the house and surprise my mother by wrapping my arms around her for a big hug.

After lunch, Mom reminds me I haven't visited Gran Nola in a while, so I hop on my bike and head for her house. As I pedal through country roads then glide down Wild Street into Sun Flower, I'm on the lookout for lost animals. Before I left home, I flipped through the stack of Lost and Found flyers Mom recently gave me. While Becca, Leo, and I keep the CCSC a secret, our families know we help reunite missing pets with their owners.

I see plenty of dogs on leashes and a few cats sunning on their porches, but no missing pets. As I slow in front of my grandmother's house, a German shepherd streaks past my bike. I squeeze my brake hard and my bike skids forward—narrowly missing the dog. I'm jerked forward, almost tumbling over my handlebars, then whipped back.

I regain my balance then stare down the street at the retreating dog. I see a glint of silver tags around its neck, so it's not a stray. Does he live nearby? Did he escape from his yard? I'm debating whether or not to go after the dog when my grandmother rushes out of her house.

"Kelsey, are you okay?" Gran Nola pushes up the sweatband holding back her shoulder-length silver-streaked brown hair as she looks closely at me. She's wearing her purple yoga pants with a Lycra top. "I was working out by the window and gasped when you nearly took a header on the pavement."

"I'm fine, but I'm worried about that dog." Biting my lip, I stare down the street. "Did you see him?"

"Yes." She nods. "He belongs to my neighbor

Greta Laszlo. Sometimes when Greta is out walking him, she stops to talk to me. It's odd to see Major without Greta. He's too well-behaved to run off."

"I'll check it out," I say and hop on my bike and go after the dog.

I reach the end of the street and hesitate. Do I turn right or left?

Left, I realize when a pickup truck slams on its brakes. The German shepherd runs across the street and dives between two parked cars in a driveway and into a front yard.

A man washing a car next door turns to stare.

"Stop that dog!" I shout.

"Come!" the man barks in a commanding tone. "Sit!"

To my surprise, the shepherd bounds up to the man, tail wagging, and promptly sits down.

"Your dog responds well to commands," the man says with amusement.

"Thanks, but he's...well...thanks for stopping him," I say, not wasting time explaining that the dog isn't mine.

I grab a leash from a compartment on my bike (I always keep one handy) and hold it behind my back as I advance toward the dog with my hand outstretched. He sniffs my fingers then gives me a big sloppy lick.

"Good boy." I wipe my hand on my jeans then bend down to read his tag: Major. So Gran Nola was right.

I snap the leash to Major's collar. Easiest lost dog recovery ever! Major regards me with trusting dark eyes and follows as I walk my bike back to my grandmother's house.

Gran has her cell phone to her ear as she greets me at the door. She takes one look at Major and gives me a troubled smile. She sets down her phone, shaking her head. "I called Greta's house but there's no answer so I left a message."

"I'll take him home," I offer. "It can't be far."

"Only two blocks. But there's no point in going there if Greta isn't home. Her son must have taken her to church. She doesn't drive anymore since her hip surgery, although that doesn't stop her from walking Major."

"He walked himself today." I pat the dog on his head. He licks my hand then tugs on the leash like he's eager to go home.

"Come, Major." Gran Nola holds open her front door for him. "You can stay here until Greta calls.

It'll be nice to have a dog in the backyard again."

Does Gran miss Handsome? I wonder, startled by the wistfulness in her voice. I'd been so happy when we moved to a house with a yard big enough for Handsome that I'd never considered my grandmother's feelings. For half a year she cared for Handsome, and she probably misses his company.

We take Major into the backyard. I find a Frisbee Handsome left behind and throw it to Major. But he walks away, pawing at the gate and whining.

"I'll take you home when Greta calls," Gran Nola says to him and pats the phone in her pocket. "Come on inside, and I'll give you a treat."

Major doesn't want a treat, but he laps water from Handsome's old bowl.

"Want to do some yoga?" Gran Nola asks me.

When I nod she places yoga mats on the floor. While I'm twisted in a crane pose, Major comes over and stretches beside us too, doing his own version of Downward Dog.

When we haven't heard from Greta an hour later, I offer to take Major home again. But Gran says to wait until we hear from Greta. Not easy for impatient me, and I can tell by the way Major keeps going over to the door that he's anxious to get home.

Gran knows I like puzzles, so we work on a one-thousand-piece puzzle mystery with clues in the images to a famous book title. The clues show up when the puzzle is finished. There are three picture clues: a hound dog, smoking pipe, and Baker Street sign.

"Sherlock Holmes lives on Baker Street," Gran Nola says, pursing her lips as she studies the emerging puzzle.

"And he smokes a pipe." I snap my fingers. "Hound plus pipe equals *The Hound of the Baskervilles*. I have that book on my shelf—"

The phone rings.

I suck in my breath. Is it Greta calling back?

"For you," Gran says as she glances at the phone screen. "Your friend Becca tracked you down—a clever little Miss Sherlock Holmes herself."

Puzzled, I put the phone to my ear. "What's up, Becca? Is everything okay?"

"Better than okay! I took your advice!" Her excited voice rises.

"What advice?"

"Remember when we talked about how much I missed Zed and you suggested I visit him?" She doesn't wait for my answer and rushes on. "When

I asked Mom, she loved the idea of a road trip for spring break. She called Zed's owner and it's all set. We're leaving in two days!"

"That's great! You'll have so much fun!"

"I can't wait to see Zed. But what if he doesn't remember me? His name isn't even Zed."

"He hasn't been gone that long." I chuckle. "He'll remember you."

"I don't leave until Tuesday so we can still have a club meeting at the Skunk Shack tomorrow," she adds. "I talked to Leo and he'll be there."

"I'm sure he will." I remember the dizzy way Leo smiled at Becca.

"Yeah, he's never late." Becca laughs. "He'll be there at 12 p.m. exactly. He's so predictable it's cute."

She says this fondly, the way she would about a cute puppy. If Leo does like her, he's going to be crushed when he realizes she doesn't feel the same way. They'll get awkward with each other. Maybe skip CCSC meetings. It could be the beginning of the end of our club.

"Becca, about Leo…" I start to say then falter.

"What about him?"

"It's just…um…well, he's younger than us."

"Duh. He hasn't had his birthday yet. He won't say when it is, but I think it's pretty soon."

I don't say anything because one of the secrets in my notebook of secrets is that Leo skipped a grade so he's more than a year younger than us. Of course, he's smarter than most adults...except when it comes to girls.

My grandmother comes over and gives me a get-off-the-phone look. "I have to go, Becca," I say, relieved to postpone this conversation.

"Okay. Talk to you later," Becca says then clicks off.

Sighing, I hand the phone back to my grandmother. My gut churns with a bad feeling—not just about Leo secretly liking Becca, but also about Greta.

"Gran, still no answer?" I ask after she tries calling again.

"No." My grandmother's gaze falls on Major who paces by the front door.

"No more waiting." She walks to the coatrack and slips on a coat. "Let's go on a walk."

"Yes!" I jump up and clip the leash back onto Major's collar.

Outside the weather has turned windy and the

sky is filled with rolling gray clouds. Major barks impatiently and pulls on the leash, tugging me forward. It's obvious he wants to run faster than the gusting wind, but he keeps a steady pace on the leash.

"Make a right turn on Melody Lane," Gran Nola says as she hurries to catch up. But I don't need her directions. Major knows where he's going.

When we reach a blue house with tidy rows of flowers blooming up to the porch, Major whines and looks back at us with pleading eyes, like he's trying to tell us something. There's no car in the driveway, but that makes sense since Greta doesn't drive. Major tugs us to the front door.

Gran rings the bell, and we wait.

I listen for the sound of footsteps but no one answers.

Major whines plaintively and paws at the door.

Gran calls loudly for Greta. I pound on the door, calling along with her. No one answers so I twist the knob. The door falls open. Gran and I exchange worried looks, and she steps boldly into the house.

"Greta!" she calls out. Her gaze sweeps across the living room and down the hall. "Are you here?"

My heart skips when I look at the glass-topped coffee table. "Her purse."

"And there's her cane," Gran Nola adds, pointing to one propped against the wall.

Major barks frantically. He jerks forward so fast, the leash slips from my hand. He bolts around the corner, through the living room and into the kitchen—which is where we find Greta—crumpled on the floor.

- Chapter 13 -
SOS!

I've never been so relieved to hear the shrill squeal of an ambulance.

Uniformed paramedics rush into the house and Greta is carried out on a stretcher to the ambulance. She's alive but just barely. A paramedic questions my grandmother but Gran Nola doesn't know much except the first name of Greta's son and that he's a dentist. We find his number in Greta's cell phone. After a terse conversation, Gran Nola and I clutch hands, watching the ambulance roar away, sirens blaring.

"She'll be all right," Gran Nola assures me, but her brow furrows in worry lines. "Her son is on his way to the hospital."

"What about Major?" The dog stares down the street, whining. "He can't stay here alone."

"He won't." My grandmother pats the dog on his head. "I told Greta's son I'd take care of him. He's a great dog and I have a big, empty yard. Until Greta's home, he can stay with me."

Later that night, Gran Nola calls the house with good news. Although Greta has a concussion from losing her balance while getting up from a chair and will have to stay in the hospital for a few days, she's going to be fine.

Relieved, I fall asleep rereading *The Hound of the Baskervilles*.

I sleep in the next morning, lingering beneath my warm covers and I cuddle my slumbering kitten. Usually on a Monday I'd jump out of bed early, get dressed, eat a quick breakfast, then bike off to school.

But it's spring break and I enjoy a delicious feeling of possibilities. I have a secret tree house, a purring kitty beside me, and great friends who love to solve mysteries. The CCSC isn't meeting until noon so I can be lazy in my bed all morning if I want. It's very tempting to stay here.

When knobby branches tap against my window like tiny paws, I think of the ferret. Is Bandit in the tree house or is she with the kitty crowd at Sergei's house? She probably belongs to Sergei, but what if she doesn't? I have to ask Sergei...actually talk to him, which is scary.

Gnawing at my lip, I stare out the window, working up my courage. Sergei might not even be there. But if I'm lucky, I might catch him feeding the cats.

As I pull out a pair of jeans and a blue striped shirt, I spot something on my desk — the coded page from the tree house. After all the drama at the castle, following the ferret, and finding Greta, I'd forgotten the cryptic code. It must be an important message since it was in the pouch. But what does it say?

Peering at the odd symbols, I get an itchy sense of recognition. There's something familiar about the angled lines and random dots. Where have I seen this type of code before?

I scan the bottom shelf of my bookcase for cryptogram and coding books. Memory clicks into place and I reach for *Challenging Cryptic Codes*. I flip through the pages until I come to a chapter on cryptograms, and there it is!

"Pig Pen Code," I murmur as I study the diagram.

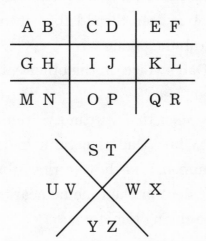

Second letter add • dot

$A =$ ⌐ $B =$ •⌐

Knowing the type of code is a good start. Slowly words take shape. The three-letter word is "the." Knowing t, h, and e helps reveal the first and last words, "beware" and "thief." The message reads:

Beware the little thief.

Does he mean Bandit? I think of her nest of twigs, clothes, and other found objects.

I'm on my way outside to find a ferret but only make it to the kitchen when the phone rings. I pause, expecting someone else to pick up. *Where is everyone?* I wonder when the phone keeps ringing.

"Drats," I mutter then detour into the living room and grab the phone.

"SOS!" Dad's voice on the other end rises with panic. "I need help!"

"What happened?" My fingers tighten around the phone. While Dad is careful in the kitchen, accidents happen. Like the Cherries Jubilee flaming eyebrow incident or the time he nearly cut off his pinkie while slicing tomatoes.

"Herb emergency!" he says in a rush.

"Huh?" I sink to the couch. "How can herbs be an emergency?"

"I'm planning a lunch of herb-encrusted chicken with creamy leak sauce but I need my own herbs and I can't leave to get them because soup is simmering on the stove," Dad explains. "Can you bring them?"

"Sure," I say, always glad to help Dad, and maybe I'll run into Sergei.

He rattles off a list of herbs and also asks for his carved redwood salt and pepper shakers. His kitchen is very organized so it doesn't take long to gather everything into a bag, and I head over to the castle.

As I pass the tree house, I glance up, half-expecting to see Bandit peering down at me. But there's no sign of life, not even a breeze to rustle the leaves.

I hear a noise, though, from the far side of the house and spot Mom knee deep in dirt and weeds. The patch of dirt she's weeding doesn't look like much now but in a few months I know it'll bloom with garden life just like our last house. Even when we lived at the apartment without a yard Mom grew plants. When it comes to nurturing living things — plants, animals, and kids — Mom has a green thumb.

"Mom, I'm going to the castle," I call out. "Dad called with an SOS."

"What's wrong?" Jumping up, she pushes a dark-brown curl from her face, leaving a smear of dirt on her cheek.

"Dad needs his herbs." I lift up my arm to show her the bag. "You know how he freaks out when he doesn't have the right ingredients."

"Total meltdown," Mom agrees, smiling. "That's sweet of you to help him."

"I don't mind. I know how much this job means to him—and all of us—and don't want anything to go wrong. Oh, and you have dirt on your face." I grin then hurry off on the path to the castle.

I rap the knocker, wondering if Sergei is already at work in the castle.

But it's not Sergei who answers the door. Perky is the word that comes to mind when Angel grins, looking adorable in a pink shirt with a sparkly hair clip shaped like a halo on her purple head.

"Kelsey, what a nice surprise to see you again! Wasn't the other night so fun? You have the sweetest family. What can I do for you?"

"I'm here to see my dad," I say.

"He's in the kitchen. I'll show you the way." She ushers me into the marble-floored foyer.

"Thanks. Isn't it the housekeeper's job to answer the door?"

"Sergei is a great housekeeper but not so great with people," she says with a shrug. "Mr. Bragg prefers that Irwin or I greet his guests."

"You and Irwin are really nice." *Unlike Sergei*, I think to myself.

"Irwin is way nicer than me. He's always giving me gifts for no reason." She tilts her head so the angel halo sways. "He's like my little brother."

"Little? He's at least a head taller. And isn't he older than you?"

"Only in years." The halo wobbles again as she shrugs. "I may not look tough, but I grew up in a rough area and had to work my way through college while Irwin lived a sheltered life of private schools and gated communities. But he'll have to toughen up when he takes over his uncle's company someday."

I'm startled by the disapproving edge to her tone. As the executive assistant, she probably knows more about the resort business than Irwin. But one day he'll be her boss. "Would you rather run the company?" I ask.

"Me? No thank you!" Her bracelets jangle as she waves my words away. "Mr. Bragg has to juggle so many responsibilities, it's no surprise he often forgets where he leaves his keys or cuff links. But he's ruthless when it comes to negotiations. Irwin is the total opposite. He's not cutthroat enough to survive in the business world."

"Irwin is really smart, so he'll learn," I say, not sure why I feel the need to defend him. Maybe because he reminds me of Leo.

"But Irwin is more artsy, crafting angel wings

on my shirts and this cute hair band." She adjusts the halo. "He's always doing things for others. He took care of his mother—Mr. Bragg's older sister—after her third divorce then dropped everything to move here when his uncle asked for help. He's just way too nice." She says this like being nice is a bad thing, but it boosts my respect for Irwin.

Angel points to the bag I'm holding. "What's in there?"

Glass containers clink against one another as I lift up the bag. "Dad's herbs."

She sniffs then draws back with a puckered face. "Whew! Strong enough to knock you over." As she straightens up, the light catches her ears and green flower earrings shine like emeralds. My thoughts climb four flights of stairs to the toy room.

"Love your earrings." I try to sound casual. "Are they emeralds?"

"Jade." Angel reaches up to her ears. "I picked them up on a business trip to China. Did I mention how much I love my job? I don't need a guy to buy me gifts—I can buy my own."

"Cool." I smile. "You must know a lot about jewelry."

"More than you do obviously. You're accessory

naked! No necklace, earrings, or even a ring." She looks at me as I'm an oddity in a freak show.

I could explain that I'm a no-fuss jeans and sweatshirt kind of girl and only wear jewelry on special occasions. But I want her to confide in me. Like *Spy Techniques*, one of my favorite books, advises: Create a bond of common interests during interrogations. So I say, "I wore a silver crescent-moon necklace when I was in the Sparklers."

"Sparklers, huh?" She grins. "Sounds like my kind of club."

"Not exactly a club. It's just some girls who hang out and work on fund-raisers to help our school." This isn't the whole story of course. I was only temporarily a Sparkler so I could help Becca with the Humane Society fund-raiser. I was glad when it was over and I returned my "loaned" Sparkler necklace. Since then I haven't bothered much with jewelry. A spy prefers not to be noticed.

"With your creamy peach skin and maple-blond hair, you should wear sapphires or diamonds," Angel says as she studies me. "What's your birthstone?"

"Aquamarine."

She claps her hands. "I know just the thing! Come with me."

"Um…" I gesture toward the bag in my hand. "Dad's waiting for his herbs."

"He can wait a few more minutes."

Angel whisks me up two flights of stairs, turning left down a long hall she says leads to the wing of bedroom suites. Angel's room is spacious with a living room, a kitchenette, a deck overlooking the garden, and a bathroom. The carpet, walls, and furniture are hues of pale ivory and silvery gray. Angel strides over to a large mahogany wardrobe and flings open the double doors. It's not a wardrobe for clothes—it's the largest jewelry box I've ever seen. Necklaces, bracelets, and chain belts hang from hooks above narrow drawers probably holding rings and earrings. Angel pulls out a dime-sized turquoise heart dangling from a gold chain.

"For you!" she says.

"I can't accept something so valuable," I protest, but she's already fastening it around my neck.

"Nah, it's an imitation. I keep my expensive jewelry in there." She taps the bottom drawer then adjusts the necklace around my neck. "Perfection! It was made for you. Take a look." She marches me over to a full length mirror nearby.

The heart gem shimmers delicately. She's right—

it is perfect for me. No wonder Irwin sews angels on her clothes. Angel isn't just her name—it's her generous personality.

I'm here on a mission, I remind myself.

"I can't believe this necklace isn't really aquamarine," I say. "If you hadn't told me it was fake, I'd think it was as real as the emerald and ruby chess set."

Angel gasps. "Who told you about that?"

"Irwin." I smile innocently. "The toy room was the best part of his tour."

"What was he thinking?" Angel throws up her hands. "For a smart guy he does some really dumb things. He knows the toy room is off-limits to kids."

"I'm not a little kid. I'm thirteen," I huff as if I'm insulted. But I'm secretly pleased she's rising to my bait. "Why does Mr. Bragg hate kids?"

"He doesn't hate them. He just doesn't understand them." Angel's halo slips to a crooked angle as she shakes her head.

"Didn't he have any kids of his own?"

"Personal questions can be dangerous around here. If you value your father's job, don't ask any more." Angel takes off her halo and dangles it from her multi-ringed hand. "Most families have skeletons in their closets—dark secrets they hide from everyone else. Mr. Bragg's skeletons are barbed and explosive. I hope he doesn't find out Irwin showed you the jewel chess set."

"Irwin didn't show it to me," I say quickly. "I found it by accident then asked Irwin, and he told me the king was stolen."

"He never should have told you." Her shoulders go rigid, as if her embroidered angel wings hardened to stone.

"Why didn't Mr. Bragg just buy a new emerald king?" I persist.

"He's a purist when it comes to his collection— no replacements or replicas." Her glossy pink lips pucker as she closes the jewelry box. "Forget you saw the chess set and *never* mention it to Mr. Bragg. It's a very painful subject."

"Irwin said the same thing. But what's so painful? I mean, Mr. Bragg has a lot of beautiful things. Why is this theft a big secret?"

"The circumstances were disturbing." She glances around uneasily as if afraid of being overheard. "He was betrayed by someone he loved."

I stare at her in surprise. "You know who stole the emerald?"

"Of course I do. That's why the theft was never reported. The day the emerald king disappeared, Mr. Bragg lost more than a chess piece." She twists the halo in her hand, her expression haunted with sadness. "He lost his family."

Chapter 14

The Cat Guy

Angel refuses to say more, and hurries me out of her suite.

As we wind down the staircase, my head spins with questions. What family member did King Bragg lose? The only family I know about is a sister and his nephew. Is Mr. Bragg married? Divorced? Widowed? Does he have any children? And why not confront the person who stole the emerald king and demand it back? Why all the secrecy?

When I smell the sweet aroma of pastries and cinnamon, I know we've reached the kitchen even before Angel opens the door and pushes me inside. She leaves so fast the door slams behind her.

"I've missed you so much!" Dad rushes toward

me with outstretched arms. But instead of putting his arms around me, he grasps the herb bag.

"Glad to see you too, Dad," I tease.

"Thanks for bringing my herbs, Kelsey. Not having the right ingredients is like working blindfolded without hands." Dad arranges the herb containers on the marble island. "I owe you big time. Would you like an apple crumble muffin—fresh from the oven?"

I never say no to Dad's muffins. When I take a bite, sweet cinnamon and apple melts in my mouth. As I eat, I admire Dad's new kitchen. It's as big as a classroom with three ovens, two refrigerators, floor-to-ceiling dark-wood cabinets, and a marble-topped island.

"Impressive, huh?" Dad smooths a wrinkle on his starchy formal white apron.

"Very cool. It must be fun working in a fancy castle."

"It's not an authentic castle," Dad says. "It's just a large house with battlements and turrets. And this kitchen looks pretty, but it lacks necessities like herbs. I did find salt and pepper shakers, but they belong in a museum, not a kitchen. Mr. Bragg has very expensive taste." Dad opens a cupboard and pulls out cut-crystal salt and pepper shakers.

"Ooh!" I say. "Sparkly."

"There are diamond encrusted S and P symbols on the silver caps."

"Wow! Can I hold one?"

"Be careful," Dad says as he hands me the S shaker.

I cradle it carefully, running a finger over the pointy edges. My Sparkler friends would be impressed. "Pretty but I'd be afraid to use them," I say as I hand the shaker back to Dad.

"Exactly why I won't use them." Dad puts the crystal shakers aside then reaches into the bag I brought and pulls out his wooden shakers. They're dented, shabby, and stained, but he holds them with a loving expression. "If I drop one of these it won't shatter into a diamond disaster."

I chuckle then get serious. "Dad, can I ask you something?"

"For a bigger allowance?" he jokes.

"Not what I had in mind, but can we talk about that later?"

He laughs. "Spit it out, Kelsey. What's on your mind?"

"When we toured the castle last night I didn't

see any pictures of Mr. Bragg's family. In our home there are photos of us kids plastered all over the walls. Doesn't Mr. Bragg have any family?"

"You met his nephew." Dad sets his wooden shakers on a windowsill behind the porcelain sink. "And he has a sister, Irwin's mother."

"No wife or kids?" I ask.

"Hmm...I heard he has an ex-wife." Dad picks up his well-thumbed, four-inch thick cookbook. "But when I was hired, I was instructed not to ask personal questions. And I don't want you doing it either."

Dad knows me too well. Fortunately there are other ways of finding things out without asking questions. There must be a gazillion websites with information on the King of Resort Hotels. I'll check online when I get home.

"Thanks for the muffin," I say, licking cinnamon off my lip.

"Thanks for answering my SOS. These cupboards aren't well-stocked." Dad opens a tall double-door cabinet that has only a jumbo bag of flour, two wine bottles, and several sardine tins. "I'm making a long list for Sergei for the next time he goes grocery shopping."

"Sergei does the shopping?" My ears perk with interest.

"He oversees the running of the household," Dad says. "Actually Sergei acts more like my boss than Mr. Bragg. I report to Sergei with my daily menu. But he hasn't shown up today. He comes and goes as he pleases."

"I don't like him." I make a bitter face. "He was rude and grumpy at dinner."

"He's not very talkative," Dad admits. "But he's a hard worker and treats me fairly."

"He's nicer to animals than people. I saw him feeding over a dozen cats."

Dad gives a low whistle. "I didn't peg him for the cat-lady type."

"More like a cat guy." I grin.

"Good to know he has a soft side." Dad leans in to whisper. "To be honest, I thought he was a grump too."

Dad laughs and I enjoy the sound, because for half a year, after losing his job at Café Belmond, he rarely smiled or laughed. I heard Mom talking to a friend, and she said Dad was depressed. I hope this job lasts a long time.

I give Dad a hug good-bye and hurry out of the

castle, eager to get home and find out about Mr. Bragg. I think of Angel saying, "He lost his family." How does someone lose a family? People don't get misplaced like keys or shoes. Did she mean "lost" like they died, maybe in a tragic accident? Or did they mysteriously vanish? Mr. Bragg must have more relatives than a nephew and sister. And one of them must have stolen the emerald king.

I'm puzzling over this as I leave the castle, not paying much attention while I hurry down the steep steps—when a flash of gray on the lawn catches my eye.

A small animal scampers across the paved path.

Bandit! I recognize the masked pointy face. In her mouth is something silver and floppy—Angel's halo hair band!

This all happens in a few blinks—the ferret scampering, the silver flash of the halo—then Bandit disappears into leafy bushes.

I have to get her headband!

Running, I keep my gaze on the sculpted bushes bordering the lawn like a moat. Then I see it—a curve of gray tail, then it's gone again. The bushes are almost as tall as I am and too thick to jump over. Bandit pops out like a target in a video game, in and out, back and forth, as if she's purposely leading me on a wild ferret chase.

Is this a game to her? I wonder as I run down the pathway curving around to the back of the castle.

When I call out, "Bandit!" she speeds up. So I run faster too, jumping over a decorative bench and dodging a planter of blooming spring flowers. I keep one eye on the blur of gray and the other on the ground to avoid tripping. I'm racing through a garden I don't recognize because I'm not familiar with this side of the castle.

Even before I see the peaked-roof, I've guessed where Bandit is leading me—to Sergei's house.

With each step closer, my heart pounds. I want to be a brave spy, fearlessly pursuing clues and suspects, but Sergei is one intimidating dude. He may like cats but I don't think he likes people much.

Instead of feeling brave, I really want to turn and run home.

But I chase after Bandit. She dives off the path and I follow—until I round a corner and stop in front of Sergei's house.

The house is dark. But the sun streaks through gray clouds, brightening the yard where empty cat food dishes are scattered across the lawn.

A streak of gray jumps onto the porch.

I chase after the ferret, running so fast I forget to watch where I'm going. A decorative boulder looms before me. I spring up to jump...too late.

Thwack! My leg smacks against the rock. I stumble backward, landing on my butt.

Pain spikes through my leg. If my knee had a voice it would be screaming.

Wincing, I close my eyes and when I open them again, I'm looking up into a metal-pierced face.

Sergei.

- Chapter 15 -
Pawn

"You hurt?" Sergei's deep voice rolls with his accent.

"Um...I'm okay." My heart quakes and my knee stings. I look down at the hole in my jeans.

"You're bleeding."

"Not much." I try to push myself up with my hands but pain knocks me back to the ground.

"You come with me," Sergei commands.

"No!" I cry, panicked. "I have to...ouch...get the halo."

"Halo?"

"Angel's headband."

He frowns as if he's trying to figure out what species of human I am. "Now I remember you.

You're the cook's daughter," he says in careful English, and from his accent I guess he's Russian.

"Yes, I was just talking to my dad in the kitchen." I gesture toward the castle. "He knows I'm headed home. My mom will be expecting me soon. I really have to go..."

"Your da...I mean, your father...he is a fine cook. I much enjoy his food."

"Yeah, he's great. But I have to get the headband before it's chewed up by the"—I hesitate—"by an animal."

"A cat?" The arrow-shaped rings in Sergei's brows seem to be aimed at me as he furrows his forehead. "There are many around here."

"I know. I saw you feeding them."

"Hungry cats need food," is all he says with a shrug.

"It wasn't a cat, it was a ferret," I say. "She stole Angel's halo band."

"Ah, the little furry fellow is up to his tricks again." Sergei's frown lifts at the edges, the closest I've seen to a smile.

"Not a he; the ferret is a girl," I correct him. "She plays with my kitten sometimes and she has a nest in...near my house. My friend Becca knows a lot about ferrets and told me that female ferrets collect things to make nests. I don't know how she got the headband but I have to return it to Angel," I rush on nervously.

He nods as if this makes sense. "I will find the band to return to Angel. The furry friend has a hiding place nearby."

"So she does belong to you?" I ask, raising my eyebrows.

"*Nyet*. I mean, no." He shakes his head. "No one owns the creatures of the wild. But the ferret likes to sleep in my shed."

"How long has she been staying there?"

"Few months." He grasps my hand. His callused fingers are surprisingly gentle as he helps me to my feet. He points to my bloody knee. "I will fix."

"I don't need to be fixed." I wobble as I try to walk.

"I will clean for you. You do not want infection."

Before I can argue, he scoops me up in his arms and carries me up the steps into his house. The door thuds behind us.

My parents have warned me not to talk to strangers—and this metal-pierced man has to be one of the strangest people I've ever met. But he's kind to animals, works with Dad, and seems concerned about my knee.

So I switch to sleuth mode and study my surroundings.

The living room is crowded with an oversized dark leather couch that probably folds out into a bed, an odd twisted-metal sculpture, and a giant TV that takes up an entire wall. But every surface is shines with cleanliness. Kudos to Sergei's housekeeping skills.

Sergei sits me gently on the couch. "You wait. I get first-aid kit," he says then strides down a hallway to the back of the house.

It's eerie being here alone.

Or am I alone? What's that sound?

A shadow moves across a recliner, and I see a long tail swish. I meet the golden gaze of a giant ginger cat as it gracefully lunges from the chair to the couch and pads over to me.

"Hello, pretty kitty." I hold out my hand for him to sniff. "Do you like to be petted?"

The answer is yes. He purrs when I scratch below his chin. "I have an orange cat too," I tell him. "But my kitten is only a few months old and about the size of your head. My, you're a big kitty."

"Alexei is a Maine coon," Sergei's voice comes from behind me. "He weighs over twenty pounds."

"Wow! That's a lot for a cat."

I pull my hand away from Alexei but he reaches out to paw me.

"He will not want you to stop," Sergei says, and for the first time he's smiling. His teeth are smallish and a little crooked.

He bends down to swab dirt away from my knee with a soft damp cloth.

"Thanks...ow!" I flinch as he dabs on antibiotic ointment.

Sergei takes out a bandage from the kit then shakes his head. "Too small. Wait here," he says then stands abruptly and leaves the room again.

Alexei rubs up against me and I get the hint, so I pet him. He reminds of me of his owner, intense to look at but a big softy.

I hear something bang from the back of the house. Sergei must be having trouble finding a larger bandage. The bleeding has stopped so I go to tell him I don't need one. As I pass the kitchen, I notice a wall covered with framed photos.

Of course I have to snoop.

One of the photos shows Sergei as a teenager

without piercings and standing proudly in a crimson and gold school uniform. Above that is photo of a pretty red-haired girl who looks a little like him—his sister maybe. She's in another photo too, but older and cradling a baby. There's also a photo of a bushy-tailed orange kitten which must be Alexei.

As I turn to leave, a scrap of paper on the table catches my eye. It's the size of a movie ticket and seems out of place on the shining dining room table. I check it out.

The paper has a serrated edge like it's a receipt ripped off a larger piece of paper. At the top in bold print, there's a numbered code, the name *S. Petrov*, a February date, and a money amount: $1,250.00. The small print at the bottom reads Paul's Pawn Shop.

A pawn ticket!

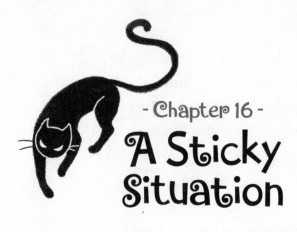

- Chapter 16 -
A Sticky Situation

My knee is bandaged, my jeans are ruined, but all I can think about as I limp home is the pawn ticket. On crime shows, thieves often pawn stolen items. A startling suspicion strikes me. The emerald king was stolen about three months ago. If the entire set is worth about $85,000 (according to Leo's calculations) then one chess piece would easily be worth a thousand dollars.

Could the emerald king be at Paul's Pawn Shop?

Shaking my head, I pause to lean against a tree. My knee doesn't hurt much but walking fast might start the bleeding again. I think back to Angel hinting that a family member stole the chess piece, which rules out Sergei. He's not in the Bragg family.

Still, the pawn ticket is suspicious, and I can't wait to discuss it with my club mates.

I have an hour before our CCSC meeting, so when I get home, I hunker down in front of the computer. I can hear Mom running the vacuum upstairs and my brother watching TV in the living room. My sisters aren't around. They're probably still avoiding each other.

When I Google the "King of Resorts," I find out his full name is Franklin Dickson Bragg, but I can't imagine anyone calling him Frankie, like our associate CCSC member's nickname.

I click a link that sends me to a travel website. Other links turn out to be advertisements too. I try more specific word combinations—and bingo! There's a photograph of a much-younger Franklin Dickson Bragg with his arm around a stunning dark-haired woman. She has warm dark skin and smiling glossy-peach lips. Her name is Jasmine Simone. The caption reads, "King Chooses His Queen." A wedding announcement dated from thirty-eight years ago. I do the math and realize Mr. Bragg is over sixty. If he has kids, they're old enough to have kids of their own.

Another link mentions Jasmine twelve years

later: a divorce announcement. I skim over the article, which is mostly boring legal details, until I reach the last line: *Jasmine Simone-Bragg maintains custody of their daughter, Deidra.*

Mr. Bragg does have a child! At least she was a child when the article was written over two decades ago. Did Deidra have regular visits with her father like Leo does with his dad? Or did she grow up without him? Even an estranged father would talk about his daughter, not pretend she doesn't exist. I remember Angel saying the emerald king's theft ripped the Bragg family apart.

Did Mr. Bragg's ex-wife or daughter steal the emerald king?

I glance at my watch and jump up from the computer. Only ten minutes to get to the Skunk Shack! I lose two minutes powering down our ancient family computer, but I make up time by biking super fast to our clubhouse hidden in the woods at Wild Oaks Sanctuary.

Leo's gyro-board and Becca's bike are already parked outside the Skunk Shack when I roll up. I prop my bike against the flat stump that we sometimes use as a bench.

"Kelsey, I'm so glad you're here!" Becca hurries

out of the shack. She's in all black today, leggings under a zebra-striped short skirt and black ankle boots with pink laces to match the pink streak in her black ponytail.

I glance over her shoulder into the shack. "Where's Leo?"

"Good question." A strong breeze blows Becca's striped bandanna in her face. Pushing it back, she frowns. "He's hiding."

"Hiding?" I peer into the thicket of trees surrounding us.

"Actually he's waiting for us to hide so he can find us. It's a spy game, like when you had me piece together a ripped letter and Leo escaped from locked handcuffs. He left these behind with a note." Becca opens her palm to reveal two of Leo's latest inventions: colorless sticky bubbles.

The spy game is on!
1. Attach a sticky GPF to your clothes.
2. Hide in the woods.
I will find you.

"But he won't find us," Becca says mischievously. "We'll fool him by hiding together—in a place he'll never find."

I love her evil grin. Leo thinks he's so smart but not this time.

I pick up one of the GPFs and look for a pin or something to stick it to my clothes. I don't see anything but when I hold it, there's a tingly sensation like electric energy and I drop it...only it never hits the ground. The sticky ball lands on my leg and sticks there like an unseen force is holding it.

"Coolness," Becca says, her GPF stuck to her bandanna.

She leads me away from the Skunk Shack. We don't go far, just over a stream and around some wild berry bushes along a steep rocky hill.

"Where to now?" I look around for an easy path through the prickly brush and towering rock formation.

She points to the rock.

"No way," I protest. "Even if we can climb up there, we'll be easy to spot, and Leo will find us."

She slides around the rock, feeling along a crevice with her hand, pushing aside berry vines and then suddenly she's not there. I blink, moving down along the rock the way she went, careful of the thorny vines—until an arm reaches out and

Becca grabs me. Only then do I see that behind the vines is a narrow space in the rock that widens into a brilliant hiding place.

Becca is right—Leo will never find us.

So we follow Part 2 of his instructions and wait.

"What do you think this GPF does?" Becca whispers.

"No clue," I whisper back, unable to see Becca in the dark space, but I can smell her lemony shampoo. "It's doesn't light up or have any wires."

"It's not a camera or listening device," she says.

"It's sticky like Velcro." I reach down to touch the spongy bubble on my leg.

"It must do something interesting like the drones," Becca guesses. "Leo comes up with amazing inventions. He's the smartest guy I know."

"So you like him?" My whispered words linger like an echo.

"Well, sure." She sounds surprised. "Don't you?"

"Of course."

"Sometimes you argue with him," she points out.

"Only when he's got a know-it-all attitude."

"But he *does* know a lot," Becca says.

"That doesn't make it less annoying." I sigh into the darkness. "He's smart with facts but clueless with feelings—even his own. He wanted to tell me something the other day but then he changed his mind. And lately I've noticed..." I falter, my cheeks warming. "I mean, he likes you a lot."

"Good," she whispers. "I like him a lot too."

"You do? But I thought you liked Trevor."

"Like isn't the same as *like*."

The funny thing is, I know what Becca means.

"When I'm near Trevor my heart gets all jumpy," she adds with a giggle. "And I wonder if he likes me too. But that's not the same way I like you and Leo. Club mates are the best kind of friends."

"The very best," I say and wonder if Becca can tell I'm smiling even though we can't see each other.

"Helping animals in the CCSC makes me feel good." She reaches out to squeeze my hand. "Better than an A on a test or getting a gift. It's like I'm giving a gift of myself and what we're doing really matters."

I think of our three kittens, Zed the zorse, the Aldabra tortoise, and all the lost animals we've reunited with their owners. "The CCSC matters," I agree.

"And we have so much fun finding lost pets, having club meetings, and doing things like spy games—even when we're squished inside a rock." Becca giggles. "It's never boring around you and Leo."

"I feel that way, but I'm never sure what he's thinking," I add more seriously. "Leo has a different way of looking at things. And lately he's been acting more awkward than usual. I think he may...well... that he may like one of us more than a friend."

"Oh!" Becca gasps. "Now I understand!"

"Good." I sigh with relief. "I wasn't sure how to tell you."

"You can tell me anything, Kelsey."

"I know...it's just that this isn't easy to talk about...I mean I worry that things will get weird between us."

"No worries," she assures me. "Nothing you can say will change our friendship. I think it's sweet that Leo has a crush on you."

"Me?" I choke out.

"I'm not surprised. You're both smart and interested in scientific stuff," she goes on. "And I've seen the way you look at him when you think no one's looking."

"But I don't! That's not what I—" I'm interrupted by footsteps stomping toward us.

The bushes concealing us are shoved aside.

Leo grins at us triumphantly. "I found you!"

Chapter 17

Cash, Clues, and Crushes

"The Global Positioning Finders led me right to you," Leo explains as we sit around the lopsided table in the Skunk Shack. We're sipping juice pouches and snacking on vegetable chips. Becca keeps giving me sideways grins, and I noticed that she managed to push Leo's chair and my chair closer together.

But I'm not the one he has a crush on! I want to tell her.

"Leo, you were brilliant." Becca sips her juice and doesn't seem to notice how her praise makes Leo blush.

"Thanks," he says with a goofy smile. *Poor guy has it bad for her*, I think. But what will happen when he finds out he's only in her friend zone?

"You found us so quickly," Becca says in awe.

"The GPFs transmit multiple locations simultaneously." He bounces several sticky balls in his hand and they clump together. "They emit identifying signals to my tablet."

His tablet shows a map of Sun Flower and he taps the northeast corner where we're located. Two dots, one pink and the other purple, blink brightly. "Becca is pink for the streak in her hair," Leo explains. "And you're purple, Kelsey."

I nod, wondering if he knows purple is my favorite color.

"The GPF is similar to GPS systems but instead of relaying information from a satellite, the balls feed locations to my tablet," Leo continues. "So when you hid in that cave—very clever hiding place, by the way—the map marked your locations even though I couldn't see you."

I pluck the GPF from my jeans. "Do they only stick to clothes?"

"Clothes and hair," Leo says.

"What about fur?" Becca looks with sharp interest at Leo. When he nods, she grins. "Coolness! They can help us find lost pets."

"Exactly!" Leo gives Becca a look so full of

admiration that my heart aches. *She doesn't like you that way*, I want to warn him.

"Cool invention, Leo," is all I say.

"But they're not perfected and need adjustments." He sighs. "The energy that makes GPFs stick is similar to static energy."

"Like when you rub a balloon against your hair and stick it to a wall?" Becca guesses.

"Close enough." Leo lifts up one. "According to my calculations, they last 1.13 hours, then they drop like dead bugs. Our experiment has given me data to improve this model. Thanks for being my trial subjects." Leo tucks them into a small box then lifts the pencil he uses as a gavel and taps it on the table. "I make a motion that we proceed with our CCSC meeting."

After the motion is passed and seconded, Leo reads the treasurer's report. Then he turns to me. "Kelsey, I make a motion that you take the floor." That means it's my turn to talk.

My wobbly chair scrapes against the wood floorboards as I lean forward to describe following Major and finding his unconscious owner.

"You had lots of excitement after we left you." Becca sips her juice.

"There's more," I add with a dramatic wave of my arms. "This morning Dad called me with an herb emergency so I had to rush over to the castle. On the way back, I saw Bandit running with Angel's halo headband in her mouth. When I chased her, I tripped and cut my knee. Sergei bandaged it for me." I gesture toward my leg.

Leo follows my gaze, frowning. "Shouldn't you have gone to a doctor?"

"It wasn't bad, just a little blood." I shrug. "Sergei took me to his house and took care of me. I thought he hated people but he was kind to me, like he is to animals. But he's still strange and suspicious." I tell them about the pawn receipt.

"Pawning something isn't a crime," Leo scoffs.

"What did he pawn?" Becca asks.

"I don't know. It wasn't the whole ticket, just a strip like a receipt."

Leo taps his pencil on the table, his expression thoughtful. "According to my calculations, on the average a pawned item pays 50 percent of its value. So Sergei pawned something worth over $2,000."

Becca sets down her juice so hard it sloshes a few drops on the table. "Like a missing emerald chess piece?"

"That's what I thought at first." My lopsided chair squeaks as I shift toward Becca. "But Angel said Mr. Bragg lost his family because of the theft—and Sergei isn't part of his family. I checked online and found out that Mr. Bragg is divorced, and his ex-wife, Jasmine, kept custody of their daughter, Deidra. But Mr. Bragg pretends they don't exist. So I think Deidra stole the chess piece—that's why her father didn't report the theft," I say with the satisfaction of solving a puzzle.

"Do you know when the chess piece was stolen?" Leo asks.

"About three months ago," I say.

"I'll bet it was Deidra's mother who took it." Becca purses her frosted plum lips. "Never underestimate the fury of an ex-wife. Divorces can get really nasty. When Dad told Mom he was leaving her, she dyed all his underwear pink."

"Pink?" I giggle but then think of the missing emerald king and grow serious. "It's all so puzzling. If King Bragg knows who took the chess piece, why not take it back?"

"Maybe it was lost or broken," Becca suggests.

"We may never know," Leo declares. "This is an unsolvable mystery."

"But I just solved it," I argue, annoyed.

"Guesses are not facts." Leo takes a big gulp of juice, squeezes his empty pouch, and tosses it in the garbage. "There's no point in investigating a theft when the victim is protecting the thief and won't report the crime."

I sigh because he's right. We don't know who-dun-it but Mr. Bragg does and pretends it never happened. The emerald king could be lost or broken.

"Fortunately our other mystery is very solvable," Leo adds cheerfully. "I have new information on one of the ARC kids."

"Gavin or RJ?" I ask.

"Gavin." Leo lifts his chin proudly. "The jogger gave us enough information that I was able to track down his father, Mikos Peay, and find their current address."

"Brilliant, Leo!" Becca high-fives him.

"Let's go now!" I jump up from the table, ready to hop on my bike.

But Leo is shaking his head. "It's too far to bike. Mr. Peay and his sons moved in with his parents in Truckee."

I groan. Truckee is up in the mountains, close to the Nevada border.

"I also located their phone number," Leo adds then turns to Becca. "As our social operative, you can make the call."

"I can do better than that." Becca's black eyes shine. "Tomorrow Mom and I are going to visit Zed in Nevada—and Truckee is on the way. I'll return the money to Gavin in person."

- Chapter 18 -
Dog-Gone Lucky Day

As we leave the Skunk Shack, I think of all the questions to ask Gavin. Did he, Zee Zee, and RJ build the tree house? Or did they find it? Why did they leave the tree house so abruptly? And why didn't they return for their cash, papers, and Bandit, especially?

I want to ask these questions, but there's one problem. Becca didn't invite me to go with her to Nevada.

And inviting myself would be awkward.

Leo powers up his gyro-board while Becca and I ride our bikes into Sun Flower. At least once a week we ride around looking for lost pets. My animal control officer mom gives us lost-pet flyers every week. Today there are four missing dogs, one lost cat, and a parrot on the loose.

Becca and I cover the neighborhoods around downtown while Leo partners up with Frankie to search the neighborhoods nearby. Frankie is usually too busy as the drama club's stage designer to go on lost pet rides, but there's no drama club during spring break. Leo snaps photos of the missing pet flyers then rides off to meet with Frankie. Becca and I study each flyer and tuck them in the compartment on my bike.

We've only been riding a few blocks when we spot a collie on his own sniffing a fire hydrant. He matches the description on one of the flyers for Pal, a two-year-old Collie-mix that escaped when a backyard gate was left open. He's been missing since Saturday.

Catching a lost dog seems like it might be easy, but not even. We've developed a five-strategy plan:

1. Call out the animal's name in a gentle but firm voice.
2. Determine if the animal is friendly or hostile.
3. If friendly, offer it a treat and clip on the leash.

4. If hostile, report the location and wait for
   official help (Mom).
5. Always proceed with caution and kindness.

Pal hikes his leg on the hydrant, unaware that Becca and I are closing in on him. The capture turns out to be easy-peasy. I barely call out "Pal" before the dog gallops toward me, wagging his tail. He almost knocks me down as he jumps into my arms. Becca attaches a leash as I offer a bacon treat, which Pal gulps down in one big swallow.

Becca pulls out her cell and ten minutes later the owner drives up. The beefy and balding guy is so happy to see his dog that he sobs big sloppy tears, hugging Pal like he'll never let go. I can't stop smiling. Reuniting people with their lost pets is the best feeling ever.

Usually we ride for hours before finding a lost pet, but today must be our lucky day. Minutes later, we spot the missing cat sniffing around a trash can at Galena Park. Capturing a cat is never easy. So instead of going after the cat, Becca contacts the number on the flyer and reports our location. We keep an eye on the cat, ready to split up and follow if needed, but the cat is still prowling around the trash can when her owner arrives.

Becca texts to update Leo and Frankie and finds out they returned the missing parrot. Three pets in one afternoon!

And the day just gets better.

As Becca gets ready to ride home, she gets a text from her mom.

"Finally!" Becca exclaims with a squeal. "Mom said yes!"

"Yes to what?" I clasp my handlebars, balancing on the sidewalk.

"You're going with us tomorrow," she says with a shrug like I should have guessed this.

"To visit Zed?" The cars zooming by are a blur as I stare at Becca incredulously. "You want me to go with you?"

"Of course! I couldn't invite you without checking with Mom. I've been waiting hours for her reply. She said yes and already cleared it with your mom. Leo's invited too." Becca pauses to send a text and within seconds her phone dings with a reply. "Leo says can't go. He's spending the day with his dad."

That night, I go to bed early because I can't wait to leave in the morning. My clothes are set out for the road trip: black jeans with zippered pockets, a purple shirt with a unicorn on the front pocket, and my winter jacket because Becca warned me it can drop to below freezing at night in Truckee if it snows.

I wake up before my alarm goes off the next morning. I get dressed quickly then head for the tree house to get the pouch with the money.

But as I lift the trapdoor, I stare in surprise.

The ferret is back!

Curled on a torn couch pillow, she looks little and sweet. Her whiskers twitch and she suddenly wakes up. Her black eyes stare at me. In a leap, she's off the couch and scampering across the floor. She springs on top of the cooler and escapes through the hole.

"Drats," I mutter. I wish she'd give me a chance to show her I'm a friend.

I cross over to the cooler and take out the plastic pouch. The bundled money and papers are inside just the way I found them.

"Bandit, I'm going to see Gavin," I call out on the chance the ferret is close enough to hear me. "Do you remember Gavin, Zee Zee, and RJ? I know they took care of you so you must miss them."

No answer of course.

It's hard to believe the apple-sized wall hole is big enough for my kitten and a ferret to squeeze through. Bandit could be on the other side of the hole, waiting for me to leave so she can go back to snoozing on the couch.

My gaze drops to Bandit's nest by the hole. It's messier than the last time I saw it. I wish Becca would have let me sweep it away. I pucker my nose at the musty odor. It's disgusting with bits of hair, paper scraps, and something purple poking from the top of the pile.

I bend down to take a closer look.

OMG! How did this get here?

I pick up my sister's shoe.

- Chapter 19 -
Road Trip

As I dangle the filthy shoe by its heel, my stomach twists. There's no mistaking the purple bow and satin ankle sash. Kiana bought these shoes for her upcoming prom to match her purple sequin gown. I remember overhearing my sisters arguing about the missing shoe, calling each other hateful things and swearing they'd never speak to each other again. They both accused the other of losing the shoe. They were wrong.

Bandit is the shoe thief.

But if I tell them a ferret did it, will they believe me? Or will they accuse me of lying to protect my kitten? If they tell Dad, he'll say Honey is too destructive to live with us. I'll lose my kitten—

unless I secretly return the shoe.

Clasping the ARC plastic pouch and purple shoe, I climb down the trunk ladder. I hope my sisters are still asleep so I can sneak into Kiana's room.

When I sniff the shoe, though, I realize I have a big problem. It smells like musky ferret. Taking a closer look, I see tiny bite marks on the heel.

I take a detour to the bathroom, where I find Kiana's makeup case. I use an emery board to file down the tiny bite marks until they blend in with the wood and wipe dirt from the sparkly fabric with a damp washrag. The shoe looks better...but that smell. Pee-yew!

Ah! I know just the thing.

I search the bathroom cupboard until I find Kenya's cosmetic case. I take out her favorite perfume, Air Kisses, a fragrance so flowery that I'd rather smell wet animal fur. Holding the shoe with one hand, I squirt perfume with the other. A shower of flowery stink gags me. But it's potent enough to mask the smell of ferret.

Now if I can just return the shoe without getting caught.

I tiptoe down the hall and reach for the door. I turn the knob so quietly that the only sound I hear is my thumping heart. Peeking into the room, I see the usual mess of discarded clothes sprawled across the floor. On one side of the room is my sister's bed with a sister-sized lump under the blankets.

Kiana makes a whiny sound as she turns onto her side and buries her face into her pillow. Holding my breath, I watch the subtle rise and fall of her blanket. All I have to do is cross the room to the closet and return the shoe so my sister won't know it was carried in a ferret's mouth to a tree house nest.

Okay, I tell myself. *On the count of three, I'll go.* One, two...

"Kelsey?" Kiana sits up in her bed and stares at me. "What are you doing?"

Covertly, I shove the shoe behind my back.

"Um..." I think fast. "Since Dad's working in the castle, we haven't had a hot breakfast in a while, so I'm making corn-flake French toast and wondered if you wanted any. Sorry to wake you."

"Breakfast is worth waking up for." Kiana rubs her eyes.

Carefully concealing the shoe behind my back, I shut the door and hurry to my room. I hide the shoe far back in my closet. But even with the door shut I can smell the Air Kisses perfume.

I'll have to wait to return the shoe, I think as I head downstairs to the kitchen. I'll make a great breakfast and wait till my sister is eating, then slip into Kiana's room to return the shoe.

Pleased with this plan, I gather cornflakes, eggs, cinnamon, milk, and bread. By the time I'm sprinkling cornflakes on battered bread, my sisters and my mom and my brother have joined me. While Kyle brews coffee, Mom tells stories about work, like how she chased a potbellied pig in a grocery store the other day. My sisters finish each other's sentences as they describe twin brothers that just started going to their school. They aren't glaring or ignoring each other, so they must have called a truce on the shoe fight. Kenya is showing a photo of the brothers when I hear a car honk from outside.

Becca and her mother are here!

I grab my jacket and hurry outside.

It's not until we're climbing into the Sierras that I realize I never returned the purple shoe.

Brilliant green shades of pine and fir trees border

the highway, thickening as we climb toward snowy-capped mountains. It's always fun hanging out with Becca, and her mom is cool too. They look a lot alike, both with curly black hair and full lips and shining dark eyes. They used to argue a lot because they're too much alike. But lately Mrs. Morales is really chill and smiles a lot. I have a suspicion it's because of her friendship with Sheriff Fischer.

"Almost to Truckee," Mrs. Morales says, glancing at me in the rearview mirror. "Becca, do you have the directions to your friend's house?"

"Already on GPS." Becca taps the map on her phone. She whispers to me, "Mom doesn't know about our tree house, just that we're returning papers to a friend."

"He'll be our friend fast when he sees the money," I tease.

"I hope so. He may not be happy to see anyone from Sun Flower." I know from Becca's somber expression that she's remembering that Gavin moved away after his mother went to jail.

Mrs. Morales takes the Truckee exit and Becca directs her through the snow-sprinkled touristy town. We cross train tracks then turn down a narrow road. "That's the house," Becca points out.

I follow her gaze to a white-paneled peaked-roof house with a detached garage and a lawn of rocks and cacti. Smoke puffs from the chimney, reminding us how much colder it is in the mountains than in the valley. I'm glad I brought a jacket.

Mrs. Morales waits in the car, leaning back and turning up the volume on a country station.

"You do the talking," I say to Becca as we step out of the car. "But don't mention the money until we're sure he's the right Gavin."

"Leo is almost never wrong," she says, "but it doesn't hurt to be cautious. I won't mention Gavin's mother either. It must be hard to have a parent in prison."

I nod grimly as we walk to the front door.

There isn't a doorbell, so I knock. From inside a bird squawks. Then I hear footsteps. A middle-aged man with thick black hair and a trim mustache and beard opens the door, giving us a puzzled look. "What can I do for you?"

"We'd like to see Gavin," Becca says with her sweetest smile.

"You look younger than Gavin's usual friends." He rubs his beard, clearly puzzled why we're here. "I'm his father and you're...?"

"I'm Becca and this is Kelsey," Becca says cheer-fully. "Is Gavin here?"

"Sure, sure...He could use some friends." The man's expression softens. "Gavin's not inside, though. He's around back. Just go through that gate."

He points to a paved path leading to a backyard where a tall boy with shaggy black hair stomps aluminum cans. He's older than us but younger than my brother, probably fifteen or sixteen. He's bundled in a heavy jacket, leather gloves, and snow boots. He tosses a squashed can into a box then lifts his foot and stomps a can.

"Gavin?" Becca calls out just as he lifts his leg to stomp another can.

He whirls to face us, narrowing his blue eyes like an animal that's been hurt and is wary of humans. "Who are you?" he demands.

Becca ignores his hostile tone and smiles sweetly. "I'm Becca and this is Kelsey."

"So?" He frowns. "I don't know you."

"We know about you and have something of yours." I gesture to my tote bag.

"That's not my bag. Is this some kind of trick?" He stomps down on a diet cola can. "If you weren't so young, I'd think you were more stupid reporters."

I quickly realize he probably means his family left Sun Flower to get away from the drama of his mother's arrest. To gain his trust, I reach in the bag and show him the plastic pouch.

"Where'd you get those?" He eyes us suspiciously.

"In a cooler."

Gavin's foot pauses mid-air over a can. "You've been in the tree house?"

"My family just moved into the cottage and I found the tree house."

"It was a mess!" Becca adds, puckering her nose.

"Animals got in and trashed it," I add. "When we cleaned it, we found these."

I take out the ARC papers and the bundle of cash. Gavin stands still as a wooden post, staring at my hand. Is he in shock?

"The notes, coded message, and money are all there," I assure him quickly.

"Don't want it." He slams his foot down on the can.

"But it belongs to you and your club mates," I say.

"I'm done with fake friends." He tosses the flattened can into a box. "Zee Zee was my girl and

RJ was like my brother. But when things got rough they bailed on me." He stomps a cherry cola can, flecks of red soda splashing onto his snow boot. "You heard about my mother, didn't you?"

Becca hesitates then nods. "It must be hard for you."

He clenches his jaw. "I thought they'd stick by me...but guess not." His tone is tough but his expression is wounded.

Bad enough his mother was arrested, but to also lose his friends must have been brutal. I'm afraid he'll stop talking to us, so I switch the topic. "What does ARC stand for? We guessed Animal Rescue Club?"

"Not Rescue." Gavin frowns. "Recovery."

"Animal Recovery Club," Becca says with an approving nod. "That's cool you took care of sick and injured animals. We have a club to help animals too."

"Good luck with that." He snorts then stomps another can. "ARC is over, and I've moved on. You should too."

"Don't you want to at least see the coded message?" I ask, gesturing to the papers inside the pouch.

"RJ was the one who liked solving them. Go ahead and figure it out yourself."

"Actually, I already did. It says: 'Beware the little thief.'"

"No big mystery. Bandit was always stealing pens and stuff." Gavin turns away and grabs another aluminum can. "I got work to do. Six bags of cans to smash before I can take them to the recycling center."

"We'll help you." Becca places a can under her shoe.

"Whatever." Gavin shrugs.

"We brought you cash," I point out as I reach for a can.

"That's club money. We earned it together, pet-sitting, walking dogs—once we even walked a potbellied pig."

Becca flashes him a smile. "Sounds like a great club."

"It was okay," he admits.

"How did it start?" I stomp a can but it slides away so I stomp it again.

"RJ was always nursing animals back to health and sometimes I helped him. When I started going out with Zee Zee, she wanted to help too."

"Ours happened by accident." Becca tilts her head toward me. "Kelsey helped me catch a runaway zorse."

"A zorse?" Gavin furrows his brow. "Is that a real thing?"

"Yeah, he's a zebra-horse hybrid. I'll show you." Becca taps her phone and scrolls through the pictures. "Here's one of Zed grazing in our pasture. He's great but he spooks easily and he ran into traffic. Kelsey helped me catch him and then we found three kittens in a dumpster." Becca continues with the story of how we started the club to care for the kittens.

Gavin relaxes a little, seeming less suspicious of us. "RJ's first rescue was an injured bunny," he says. "Then I found a bird with a broken wing."

"We have all kinds of birds at Wild Oaks," Becca says and describes her mother's wild animal sanctuary.

"We took care of wild animals too." Gavin reaches for a citrus soda can. "RJ's tree house was a safe place for the animals to recover. Zee Zee came up with the idea for a club and she wrote those notes. I told her we were too old to have a club but she usually got her way." He stares down at his boots. "I thought she'd stand by me...when things went bad."

"She dumped you?" Becca asks in a sympathetic tone.

"No...I beat her to it. When I explained that Mom didn't mean to break the law, you know what Zee Zee said? I'm sorry. I could tell she didn't want to be with me anymore. So I just left."

"You haven't spoken to her since?" Becca asks.

"Why bother?" Gavin scowls but there's pain in his eyes. "We don't have much in common anyway. I'm into rock-climbing and hiking. Zee Zee is a ballet dancer and she's really good. Sometimes after our meetings, we'd hang out at RJ's grandpa's house and play his old jukebox music so Zee Zee could dance."

"You miss her," Becca says softly.

"Nope." Gavin tosses a squashed can at the box but misses and it flip-flops to the ground. He wipes his sticky hands on his jacket. "The club's over."

"So you just abandoned the animals?" Becca scowls at Gavin. "Didn't you care what would happen to them?"

"There was only the ferret by then, and RJ took her with him."

"No, he didn't," I say.

"What?" Gavin reels back like my words slapped his face. "RJ would never abandon an animal."

"Did you ever ask him?" Becca accuses.

"How could I?" He spreads his arms out in frustration. "I didn't know where RJ went and he never replied to my messages."

"You were going to meet at the tree house that day," I say, remembering the soda cans, plates, and silverware scattered around the table. "RJ was expecting you."

"He was?" Gavin's eyes widen. "I tried to go to his cottage but couldn't get in the gate. The password I'd always used didn't work. Later I found out RJ and his family moved out."

"RJ left before you did?" I ask, surprised.

"When he didn't answer my texts, I figured his family didn't want me around because of what Mom did." Gavin slumps his shoulders.

A locked gate. A cottage. Our tree house.

"Did RJ live in the cottage?" I ask.

"How else could we meet at the tree house?" Gavin twists his lips in a grimace. "Then RJ just left. No texts. Nothing."

My thoughts windmill in circles going nowhere.

Mr. Bragg said the previous cook lived in the cottage until she was fired. But he also said there weren't any kids living on the estate, but RJ had lived there.

I turn back to Gavin. "Do you know why RJ's mother was fired?"

"Fired from the account firm?" Gavin wrinkles his brow.

"What? No. Fired from working for Mr. Bragg as his chef."

Gavin gives me a weird look then laughs. "She cooked for him sometimes but it wasn't her job. She's an accountant."

"So she didn't work for Mr. Bragg?" I ask, confused.

"Why would she work for her father?"

I stare at him incredulously. "RJ's mother is Deidra—Mr. Bragg's daughter?"

"Didn't you know?" Gavin kicks a rusty can aside. "RJ is the grandson of the rich and famous King of Resorts."

- Chapter 20 -
Mystery Solved?

Before we go, I try to give Gavin the ARC pouch but he still refuses. "It's not mine to keep."

"Well, it definitely isn't ours." I shove the pouch into his hands.

"Share it with Zee Zee and RJ," Becca suggests. "You must know some way to contact them."

"I guess I could try." He shrugs. "But they won't answer."

"Give them a chance." Becca says with an encouraging smile. "Good friends are worth fighting for... and forgiving."

He scowls but there's a thoughtful, almost hopeful, look in his eyes. "Can't hurt to try, I guess."

"If you hear from RJ, let me know," I add,

thinking of the emerald king.

"And let *me* know if you talk to Zee Zee." Becca gives him her cell number.

"You're such a matchmaker," I tease Becca as we walk back to the car. "You're hoping he gets back with Zee Zee."

"Gavin is still crazy about her—isn't it obvious?" Becca slips into the car and reaches for her seatbelt. "I'll text Leo to let him know we returned the money and found out about the ARC kids."

Mrs. Morales sings softly to country music from the front seat while I watch Becca text Leo. Minutes later her phone dings a reply from Leo.

Gr8 work. Mystery solved.

But is it really solved? I wonder as we drive east, where patches of snow shine from mountain peaks. Sure, we returned the papers and cash, found out how the club split up, and what happened to Gavin. But we don't know where RJ is or why his family left so suddenly.

And I wonder...

Why is it a secret that RJ is Mr. Bragg's grandson?

Why did RJ's family move out of the cottage?

Why did RJ abandon his friends and Bandit?

Trees, mountains, and sky blur by as I stare out

the window and realize there's only one logical answer: RJ stole the emerald king.

"Did you see that sign? We're in Nevada now!" Becca tugs my arm and points out the window. "We're almost there! I can't wait to see Zed. It's been forever since I've seen him."

I laugh. "It hasn't even been a month." I turn to look out the window too and imagine Zed's striped legs and shiny dark mane. It'll be cool to see the zorse again.

"I know he's happy now, but I miss him." Becca sighs.

"He'll be even happier to see you," I say, which makes her grin.

A short while later we drive onto a paved road circling up to a brick single-story house. Puddles splash from recent rain as we park in front of a yard green with cacti instead of grass. Last time we saw Zed's owner, Eloise Hunter, she was in a wheelchair. Now she steps out of the house only using a cane.

Her face lights up brighter than her silvery hair as she invites us inside. "I have tea, lemonade, and fresh cookies for you."

"Sounds wonderful," Becca's mother says.

Becca bounces back and forth in her cowgirl boots. "Can I see Zed first?"

Mrs. Hunter chuckles and leads the way to the barn.

Sun rays shine prisms through high windows, piles of hay climb to the pitched roof, and chickens cluck from a pen. I hear Zed's welcome—a whinny—before I see him. He's spunky and kicks his hooves with attitude when he sees Becca. She rushes over and wraps her arms around his neck.

It's an amazing afternoon of sweet lemonade, warm chocolate-chip cookies, and watching Becca ride Zed. She says I can ride too, but she has a better connection with him. He allows me to feed him carrots and pet him and that's enough for me.

Time gallops by as the sun sinks in the west and soon Becca is hugging Zed good-bye.

On the drive home, Becca falls asleep but I enjoy the scenery. As we pass the Truckee exit my thoughts whirl back to Gavin. We found out a lot from him, and we may have even convinced him to reconnect with Zee Zee and RJ. I'm still shocked that RJ is Mr. Bragg's grandson and probably stole the emerald king. But there's so much I don't understand. Why did RJ's family leave instead of just returning the emerald king? And why is Mr. King covering up the theft?

I'll probably never know what really happened. Leo was right—it's an unsolvable mystery because the victim is protecting the thief.

But is RJ really the thief? Maybe it was an accident and he broke the chess piece. Instead of confessing to his grandfather, he threw the emerald king away or gave the broken pieces to his parents. Still, a broken or stolen chess piece doesn't seem like a strong enough reason for a family to leave so abruptly. And why didn't RJ talk to his club mates? Would it have been so hard to send a text?

Leo and Becca may think the ARC mystery is solved, but I don't.

I must have dozed off, because suddenly I'm jerking my eyes open and Mrs. Morales is parking in front of my house.

My mother meets me at the door. Instead of asking her usual, "Did you have fun?" she grasps my hand and pulls me inside without saying a word.

Her expression is grim, like someone has died. I start to ask what's going on but she silences me with a look so severe that now I'm sure someone has died.

I follow Mom into the family room. Dad stands abruptly from his recliner when he sees me. He gives me a look so furious that I know immediately my relatives are alive. But I'm not so sure about my own longevity because if looks could kill, Dad's glare would have already struck me dead.

What have I done wrong? I think frantically.

I can't think of anything—until I smell sickly sweet perfume and see on top of the coffee table is a purple heeled shoe with a bow and satin sash.

"I can explain!" I start to say.

But Dad is shaking his head, and I hear a soft mewing. I look past the couch to a wooden pet carrier. Honey peers out through the slats, her yellow eyes sorrowful.

That's when I know the horrible truth.

I'm losing my kitten.

- Chapter 21 -
Accused

"But Honey didn't do it!" I rush over to the crate. My kitten looks so small and helpless that my heart breaks.

"She stays in there," he orders. "Your cat is a menace."

"She's innocent! Please don't blame her."

"We found the shoe in your closet and your kitten was nearby," Dad says roughly. He won't even look at me.

"Sorry, Kelsey." Mom slips her arm over my shoulder. "When I went into your room to check on your cat, I had no idea it would lead to this. I only looked in your closet because of the perfume smell. I never expected to find your sister's shoe."

"That's not all we found," Dad adds furiously. "A hole gnawed right through the wall between your room and your sister's."

"A hole!" My heart sinks.

"Don't pretend you didn't know," Dad accuses. "We're living in this house free of charge because of my employer. I warned you to keep your cat out of trouble. But now she's destroyed a wall. How many things will she destroy?"

"I swear it wasn't her. You can't send her away."

"She has to go." Dad rakes his fingers through his hair. "I just hope I can repair the wall before Mr. Bragg finds out. I can't risk any trouble— especially after what happened today."

"What happened today?" I wrap my arms around myself.

"That valuable pepper shaker went missing." Dad's shoulders sag.

I suck in a breath. "Not the crystal and diamond shaker!"

"Yes," he says quietly. "How could this happen? I know I put it away."

"You did. I saw you do it," I assure him, thinking back to yesterday.

"But the salt shaker stands alone." Dad blows

out a ragged sigh. "I'll be lucky if I have my job tomorrow. But if I do, I can't risk more trouble. The cat has to go."

Mom places her hand on my father's arm. "Honey is just a kitten. She'll be better behaved when she grows up."

"She can't stay in this house," Dad says in a strained voice. "I feel terrible about this. I don't want to...but what choice do I have? I need this job."

"We all do," Mom agrees softly, squeezing Dad's hand.

"But it wasn't Honey!" I jump up from the crate to face Dad. "She didn't chew Kiana's homework or steal her shoe or destroy the wall."

"Then who did?" Dad demands.

Both of my parents stare at me, and I realize I can't keep this secret anymore. "It was a ferret."

Mom looks at me with disappointment. "Kelsey, don't lie."

"But it's true! I saw the ferret."

"There have been no reports of a missing ferret," Mom insists.

"It's not a pet—it's wild."

"That's ridiculous! I've learned a lot as an animal control officer and know for a fact that domesticated ferrets can*not* survive in the wild." Mom purses her lips, a quiet signal her anger is building. While Dad has a short fuse and blows up fast, he loses steam quickly, Mom's anger is roused slowly like a volcano eruption.

Dad scowls at me. "Next you'll say the ferret stole the crystal pepper shaker."

"She did!" I snap my fingers because suddenly it all makes sense. "That's why only one shaker is missing. She can't carry two in her mouth."

"Stop making excuses," Mom says with a warning in her tone.

"But I'm telling the truth! Yesterday I chased Bandit while she was running away with Angel's headband."

"Bandit?" Mom echoes. "This wild ferret has a name?"

"I know it sounds weird but it's true. You can ask Sergei—he saw the ferret too."

"I will not ask Sergei anything so ridiculous," Dad snaps. "I realize you're upset about losing your kitten, but lying only makes things worse."

"But Dad—"

"*No.* I will not listen to any more of this. Take the crate up to your room—and do not let that menace out. Then get on the phone to find a home for the cat. This is her last night here."

I look from Dad's furious face to Mom's glare. They don't believe me. They won't listen. And tomorrow my cat will be gone.

Tears prick my eyes as I lift up the crate.

Without another word, I leave the room.

As my bedroom door bangs shut behind me, Honey mews. Her whiskers twitch as if she's scared. I want to release her from her crate prison but I don't dare.

"I wasn't lying," I whisper as I sink onto my bed, feeling like a dark moon eclipsed the sun and the world will never be light again. I hurt all over, angry words trampling my heart. I try not to cry but I keep thinking of Dad's furious face when he called my sweet kitten a menace.

"You're not a menace," I say to my kitten across the room. I want so badly to hold Honey, to tell her everything will be okay. But will it?

I think back to when Becca, Leo, and I rescued the three kittens. We each chose a kitten for our own. I fell in love with fluffy, orange, stub-tailed Honey. The kittens were so tiny and fragile, and I wasn't sure they'd survive. But they thrived under our care and a few weeks later Leo took his kitten Lucky home. Not long afterward, Becca's mother let her keep Chris too. I was the last to keep my kitten, and now she has to go.

I bend down to the crate and reach my fingers through the slates to pet Honey's soft fur. She mews up at me, begging to be let out. A lump burns in my throat. I try not to cry. *Honey will be fine*, I tell myself. Maybe she can live with Becca again and play with Chris all day. She'll love that...but she won't be with me.

A tear drips down my cheek. I wipe it away.

I can't put off the call any longer. I grab the upstairs phone and bring it back to my room. When Becca answers the phone her voice is light and cheerful. "Hey, Kelsey. It's been like fifteen minutes since I saw you. Miss me already?"

Normally I'd tease back, but I need all my energy to keep from crying. I sink down on the carpet beside my kitten's crate. "Something's happened..." I swallow hard then blurt it all out—the chewed shoe, the closet wall, and losing Honey.

"But the ferret did it!" Becca cries in outrage. "Honey's too little to do that much damage. Your parents should realize that."

"They only believe what they saw—and they didn't see the ferret."

"I saw its footprints and the nest. Even if I hadn't, I would believe you."

"My parents think I'm lying to protect Honey." My kitten bats a paw through the slats and curls it around my finger. She keeps her claws in, always gentle. "Dad is freaking out because he's afraid he'll lose another job. Also a fancy pepper shaker disappeared from the castle kitchen today. I think Bandit stole it but when I told my parents they just got angrier."

"Bandit is such a thief." Becca groans. "My ferrets are male, so they don't make nests or steal stuff. But we had a female once and when we let her play in the house she stole clothes, pens, even toilet paper rolls."

"I begged Dad to ask Sergei but he refused."

"That's so unfair!"

"I know." I sigh at my imprisoned kitten. "How can I convince them the ferret is to blame and not Honey?"

"Proof," Becca says. "And I know just how to get it!"

- Chapter 22 -
It's a Trap

I wake up to a gloomy morning. Outside my window, foggy grayness tangles branches into monstrous shadows. I'm tempted to hide under my covers all day, but I'm meeting my friends soon.

As I slip on my black jeans, my scraped knee stings. That pain is nothing, though, compared to how I feel when Honey mews pitifully from behind her prison bars. I can't stand seeing her unhappy so I unlatch the crate and cradle her in my arms.

"It's not good-bye," I murmur as I kiss her whiskery face. "You won't be far away. I'll visit you at Becca's every day. It'll be just like you're still living with me...only you won't be."

Unless Becca's plan works, I think, clinging to

my only hope.

For the plan to work, Honey must stay locked in my room, and my heart breaks all over again as I return her to the crate.

Minutes later I'm inside the tree house, my spy pack propped on my shoulders. I put out sodas and some chips for my friends.

Becca arrives first, carrying a wooden crate—not a pet carrier like the one holding my kitten, but a long rectangular box with a spring to shut the hatch quickly—an animal trap.

"Mom loaned me the trap and gave me ferret kibble to use for bait." Becca places a dish inside the trap. "Bandit won't be able to resist this yummy treat."

"I hope so," I say with a sigh. "My parents won't believe the ferret exists unless they see her. We have to catch her today."

Becca squeezes my hand. "We'll catch her—not just to prove Honey innocent but because a domestic ferret needs a real home. When I told Mom about Bandit, she was shocked that a ferret was surviving on her own."

"Not exactly on her own," I say. "Sergei has been feeding her and she sleeps in his shed and this tree house."

"But she could get sick or hurt or attacked by an animal." Becca picks up a bag of chips from the table and rips it open. "Once we catch Bandit, Mom is sure she can find her a good home."

"Your mother is so cool."

"Apparently the sheriff thinks so too—they're officially dating now."

"Are you okay with that?" I raise my brows, studying her.

"It's still weird seeing them together, but I'm getting used to it. And I'm glad Mom is happy."

"At least someone is." I frown, remembering Honey's plaintive mews. "I hated leaving Honey in a crate. I hope this trap works. Once we catch the ferret and give her to your mom, I'll sweep up the nest and board the hole."

A creaking noise makes me jump. Turning, I see a blond head appear through the trap door.

"Hey, Leo. You're styling in black," Becca says.

"Thank you." He gestures to his T-shirt, jeans, and hoodie. "After a critical study of spy websites, I determined black is the appropriate color for subversive activities."

"You look like a normal kid," Becca teases.

"Almost normal," I can't resist adding. Although

to be honest, I really like his spy style. He seems older and even a little dangerous.

But the big thing on my mind is the ferret. So when Leo sits between us at the table, I suggest we go over the plan.

"It's simple," Becca says confidently. "When Bandit comes in here, she'll smell the yummy kibble and crawl into the trap. A spring will trigger, and"—she snaps her fingers—"ferret captured."

"That's great," I say. "But it could be a long time before Bandit shows up. And she won't do it while we're here," I add, gnawing on an uneven thumbnail. "She might stay in Sergei's shed all week. And next week we go back to school."

"So let's add a Plan B." Leo's blue eyes shine as he pats the bag slung over his shoulder. "Instead of waiting for her to come to us, we go find her."

"She's probably at Sergei's eating with the cats." I glance at my watch. "Finding her will be easier than catching her. She's not like a tame cat that will come running when you call her."

Becca nods. "And if we try to grab her, she could be so scared she might claw or even bite us."

"We'll track her movements with GPF," Leo says. "It'll be interesting to see how it works on animal fur."

"How do we get one on her?" Becca flips her ponytail over her shoulder. "Bandit won't stick a GPF to herself like Kelsey and I did."

"I've improved my method for attachment. Once the GPF is attached, we'll know when she steps into the trap," Leo explains.

"And when she's caught, we'll show her to Kelsey's parents." Becca reaches out to pat my shoulder. "Don't worry. You will not lose your kitten."

I nod but I'm still worried.

We don't say much as we leave the tree house and move beneath the fog-shrouded trees. Dawn streaks through the grayness but it's still hard to see where we're going. When we reach the locked gate, I zip open my spy pack and pull out my key spider. I love this tool Leo made, not just because it can pick almost any lock, but because it looks cool, all silvery with spiky keys. A few twists of metal, and the lock opens.

Up ahead a gray blur bounds through the grass. Bandit! We follow as she curves along the garden path to Sergei's house. We stop when we hear mewing.

"Wow! So many cats!" Becca whispers as we duck behind a tree.

"Over a dozen," I say.

"Fourteen, plus one ferret," Leo corrects. "If Bandit leaves, we'll know where she goes." He opens his bag and pulls out a handful of the GPF and a hollow metal tube. He pushes a GPF into the tube then aims it at the crowd of cats.

Before I can ask what he's doing, Leo clicks a button. There's a whirring sound and a rangy-looking tabby jumps. Although the GPF is practically invisible, I suspect Leo has shot one. The cat looks around, curious but not upset. With a flick of its tail, the tabby resumes eating.

"Wrong animal," Becca mutters.

"Mistakes are impetuses to discoveries," Leo says. "Success isn't achieved in one moment but in numerous attempts. I'll try again."

I hold my breath as I watch him aim the tube again. Click. The ferret pops up, swiveling around as if searching for an enemy. Her whiskery nose points directly toward our hiding place. Gray fur blurs as she vanishes into the bushes.

"GPF fail," Becca says with a groan.

"No, I succeeded. The GPF is attached to her fur." Leo taps on his tablet screen. "She can run but her red dot can't hide. See this squiggly line? It's the path between Sergei's house and the castle."

"This black square is the castle?" I squint at the screen, trying to make sense of the symbols and lines.

"The main floor." Leo trails his finger up a spiky line. "The map shows a skeletal view of buildings like an x-ray. Here are the turrets. Now back to the ground, I'm the blue dot by Sergei's house. And the red dot—the ferret—is running around to the back of the house. Hurry!" Leo takes off running and I hesitate only a moment before I follow.

The fog has lifted now, so it's easier to follow the worn path in the grass to the back of the house.

"Target sighted!" Leo calls out.

"Bandit is in Sergei's shed," I pant as I catch up with Leo. He's so fast he should be on the track team.

"We'll trap her there," Becca says, running close behind me. "Then I'll call my mom to come and help catch her."

"And prove to my parents that she exists," I add.

Leo is so focused on his tablet, he trips over a decorative rock but I grab his arm. "Watch your feet," I say with a grin. He nods but his gaze stays on the screen.

When we reach the shed, the door is open a crack.

"Are you sure she's in there?" Becca asks Leo.

"According to my map, she is." Leo points to his tablet and I peer over his shoulder trying to make sense of the web of lines and three flashing dots on the screen. I know the blue represents Leo and the red is Bandit, but what's yellow?

When I ask, Leo's cheeks burn red and he doesn't answer.

"I know!" I snap my fingers. "It's that tabby cat you tagged by mistake."

"It's of no importance." Leo turns to Becca. "You're the animal expert. How should we proceed?"

Becca moves toward the door just when I hear a heavy footstep behind us.

I turn around and see Sergei, his arms folded across his chest as he stares down at us. He seems taller than I remember and his metal piercings glint menacingly.

"Um...Hi, Sergei," I say feebly.

"You again." Sergei points to my knee. "How is the injury?"

"Much better. Um...these are my friends Becca and Leo."

Becca smiles sweetly and Leo gives a formal bow.

"Most pleased to meet you," Sergei says in his thick accent. He tilts his head toward Leo. "You look much like my nephew Hugo. Do you have Russian family?"

"Yes." Leo lifts his chin proudly. "I was named after my Russian grandfather."

Sergei nods approvingly. "What is your full name?"

I lean in eagerly, hoping to finally learn Leo's middle name.

"Leopold Polanski," he says, and I sigh with disappointment.

"A fine name." Sergei claps Leo on the shoulder then returns his attention to me. "If you are here to find Angel's headband, it has already been found."

"In the ferret's nest?" I gesture to the shed.

He nods. "Angel joined me to search yesterday and we found the headband, an earring, silver pen, and a tooth."

"A tooth?" Becca makes a face. "Gross."

"Not human—small like a rat." Sergei cracks a half smile.

"Was anything valuable found?" I think of the crystal pepper shaker.

"No. Is something else missing?" The silver arrow in Sergei's left brow rises as if aiming at me. I don't want to get Dad in trouble, so I shake my head.

Sergei gives me a doubtful look then slides the shed door open. "To make sure, I will search again."

"Don't scare Bandit!" Becca cries but Sergei is already inside.

Becca, Leo, and I crowd around the doorway and peer into the shed. It's dark, but with light from the doorway I can make out the shadowy shapes of a lawn mower, rake, and shovel. There's an earthy smell of fresh dirt and a musty ferret odor. I can also see a shape that could be a nest.

I don't see Bandit, though with all the gardening equipment, she could be hiding anywhere. I hold my breath when Sergei leans in toward the nest.

A rustling sound from the other side of the shed startles me.

I whirl around as a furry head pops up from behind the lawn mower.

"Over there!" I cry, pointing. "She has something!"

Bandit scampers toward the doorway, a red cloth waving from her mouth.

- Chapter 23 -
Shaker Shake-Up

"Kelsey!" Leo shouts as I chase after the ferret. "Wait for us!"

Glancing over my shoulder, I see Leo with his tablet in one hand and the silver tube in the other. He waves the tube like he's trying to pantomime a message and shouts something I can't hear.

But I keep running after the ferret. I have to prove to my parents she's real. A gust of wind stirs my hair as if urging me to run faster. Trees blur by and bushes reach out with twig claws to snatch at me. Bandit ducks into the red-flowered bushes. I can't see her but I follow a trail through the hedges.

I pass Sergei's house and run into the beautifully manicured garden where red and pink and yellow flowers bloom like living art. I spot Bandit, scurrying through some rose bushes. *Go back to the tree house!* I want to shout. But instead of turning into the woods, she circles around to the castle entrance.

I hear footsteps behind me. I glance over my shoulder and see Leo has almost caught up. It's amazing he doesn't trip because he's watching the screen and not where he's going.

Bandit springs onto to a trellis where bougainvillea vines up the castle wall. I can now see what she's carrying in her mouth—a sequined scarf that I'm sure belongs to Angel. The red cloth waves like a kite in the wind as Bandit scurries along the wall and leaps down to the grassy ground. She springs onto a brick planter the sequined scarf snags on a sharp-edged brick. Bandit disappears into the dark-green bushes circling the house. I've found the scarf but lost the ferret.

I grab the soft, damp scarf and pause to catch my breath.

Leo catches up to me, panting. "Why didn't you wait? You didn't have to chase Bandit. I told you I was tracking her."

"I know, but if I hadn't been chasing her, I might

not have found this!" I wave the red scarf. "I'm sure it belongs to Angel."

"Good work." He returns his focus to his tablet. "Bandit is still running. See her red dot here?"

"Yeah," I say. "What are these squiggly lines?"

"The castle's stairs. She passed them and is crossing the driveway and...and...I don't understand. How could she go there?" Leo shakes his head. "Impossible!"

"Did you lose Bandit's trail?" Becca asks, catching up to us with Sergei. She pushes back a pink strand of hair that came loose from her ponytail.

"I know *where* she is," Leo says with a bewildered expression. "But not *how* she got there."

"So what's the problem?" Becca asks.

"She's *underneath* the castle."

"That's crazy. She's a ferret, not a mole." Becca puts her hands on her hips. "Ferrets don't make tunnels."

I jump as I have an idea. "She's in the dungeon!"

Sergei frowns. "The castle doesn't have a dungeon."

"I mean, the wine cellar." I turn to Sergei. "You and Angel disturbed her nest yesterday so maybe she was taking this scarf to another nest."

"But how would she get into the wine cellar?" Sergei looks doubtful. "There is an outside cellar door but it is padlocked."

"She's a little Houdini," Becca says.

"Can we look in the cellar?" I ask Sergei, rocking impatiently on my heels.

"I will take you." Sergei rubs the stud in his pierced lip then gestures for us to follow him. "It will be quicker to go through the castle."

We follow Sergei up the entry stairs to the castle.

"There's the door knocker you told us about!" Becca squeals excitedly. "Finally! I get to see inside the castle."

Sergei holds open the door for us as we file onto the marble foyer floor. He tells us to wait in there while he gets the key to the wine cellar.

"You don't have one?" I ask, surprised. I mean, he's the housekeeper, and I assumed he had access to every room.

"Irwin keeps the key," Sergei says with a shrug. "He is working in the study with Mr. Bragg. I'll be back shortly."

While my friends admire the marble floor, gilt framed pictures, and antique furniture, I gaze at the jukebox and think of the ARC kids. Gavin said that Zee Zee loved to dance to the jukeboxes. I can almost hear the music and imagine her pirouetting on the marbled floor. They might have run up the staircase and slid down the banister—that's what I'd do if I hung out here. But mostly I'd be in the toy room.

I'm still having a hard time believing Mr. Bragg has a grandson. Why does Mr. Bragg say that Irwin is his only heir? Even if RJ stole the chess piece, he's still Mr. Bragg's grandson. Why pretend he doesn't exist?

I'm snapped out of my thoughts when I hear footsteps. Sergei is back and Irwin is with him. The last time I saw Irwin, he was in the role of castle tour guide, spouting off facts about game history. Now he's all business in a long-sleeved white shirt, black pants, and blue striped tie.

Irwin nods at me. "Nice to see you again, Kelsey. But shouldn't you and your friends be in school?"

"We're on spring break," I say and introduce Leo and Becca.

"Instead of sunning at a beach on your vacation, you want to go into the wine cellar?" Irwin asks in a joking tone. "Aren't you kids young for wine tasting?"

"This isn't about wine," I say hurriedly, impatient to go after Bandit. "We're here to catch a thief."

Becca nods. "She's hiding in the wine cellar."

Irwin's bushy brows fuse together like a fuzzy black caterpillar. "A thief?"

"Yeah," I say. "She's been stealing from my house and the castle—a shoe, headband, crystal pepper shaker, and just now she dropped this." I lift up the red sequined scarf.

Irwin takes the scarf from me, frowning. "This belongs to Angel."

"I thought so," I say, pleased to be right. "She can't resist shiny things. She went into the cellar where she probably hid more stolen stuff. We'll lose her if we don't hurry."

Irwin stares the same way my parents did when I told them about the ferret. *He doesn't believe me!* I realize with despair.

"I'm telling the truth," I insist. "We know she's in the cellar because Leo is tracking her movements on his tablet."

"The connection fades in and out," Leo admits, frowning at the screen. "But it's working now and this red dot is the thief."

"She can't help herself from stealing," Becca

says with a sigh. "It's her nesting instinct. Female ferrets can be little thieves."

"The thief is an animal?" Irwin rubs his forehead like we're giving him a headache.

"Yes, sir. There's a ferret in the castle cellar." Sergei holds out his hand. "Please, may we have the key?"

Irwin looks completely confused, and I don't blame him. He has enough to deal with after switching careers, moving in with uncle, and learning how to run a business. "Of course," he says finally. "But I have don't have the key on me. It's upstairs in my room. I'll get it."

"Thank you," Sergei says with a half bow. "We'll wait here."

Wait is my least favorite four-letter-word. I've never been good at waiting. I confess it's something I need to work on. But not right now.

"Sergei, I'll return the scarf to Angel," I say in a rush as I head for the staircase. "She's probably in her room. I'll be so quick I'll be back before Irwin."

Before the housekeeper can argue, I run up the staircase, my fingers trailing on the polished banister. I make a few turns, surprised at how quickly I've learned my way around the castle.

Angel's room is the one at the end of the hall a few floors up. The door is partially open so Angel must be inside.

But as I reach her door, I glance into the room and stare in shock.

Someone is in the room, but it isn't Angel.

Why is Irwin in Angel's room and not his own?

His back is turned toward me as he rummages through Angel's jewelry cabinet, the doors open wide like they are wings. He swears under his breath and tugs on the bottom drawer where Angel keeps her valuable jewelry. When the drawer slides open, he moves slightly and I see what he's holding in his hand.

The missing crystal pepper shaker.

Chapter 24

A Thief Unmasked

I must have gasped because Irwin looks up at me. His eyes widen then narrow. His hands knot into fists at his sides. He was so nice when we met, but now he's turned into a different person. And suddenly I'm scared.

"What are you doing here?" he says sharply.

"I-I was looking for Angel...I didn't mean to interrupt..." My gaze is on the glittering crystal in his hand. I back up and turn to leave. "I-I'll just go—"

"No!" Irwin shoves the crystal shaker into his pocket as he lunges for the door. He grabs my arm and yanks me into the room and kicks the door shut.

"Let go!" I struggle like a wild animal, hitting, kicking, and scratching.

"Stop that...ouch! I'm not going to hurt you. I'll explain, if you'll just calm down."

I answer by aiming high and kicking him hard.

He cries out in pain, doubling over, but he doesn't loosen his grip. "Just...Just listen," he gasps. "You must promise not to tell anyone I have the pepper shaker."

"I-I promise." Of course I'm lying. I'm going to blab to the world as soon as I leave Angel's room.

"I know this looks bad but it's not what you think." Irwin's shoulders sag.

I think he's a lying creep who is fake nice and steals from his own uncle. But saying that wouldn't be a smart move.

"My friends and Sergei will come looking for me." I try to pull away but he has an iron grip on my arm.

He frowns nervously at the door then back at me. "Please, try to understand that I didn't mean for this happen. Angel will be hurt if she finds out. You like her, don't you?"

"Sure, I do. And I thought you did too," I say bitterly. "But when you like someone you don't try to frame her by hiding a stolen shaker in her room."

"Is that what you think?" he asks, scowling.

"It doesn't matter what I think. Just let me leave...you're hurting me."

"I'm sorry." He loosens his grip but doesn't let go. "I would never let Angel take the blame. I like her a great deal and would do anything for her." He glances regretfully at the jewelry box. "So she must never know what I've done. Please don't tell her about my problem."

"Problem?" I stop struggling to stare at him.

"I-I can't help myself." His voice cracks and when he loosens his grip on me, I lunge for the door.

But I don't hear footsteps chase after me, only a pitiful sigh. So I pause in the doorway and glance back. Irwin's face is in his hands and his shoulders heave like he's crying. He looks broken, as if he's more fragile than the crystal shaker clutched in his hand.

"I'm sorry I grabbed you," he says softly. "It was unkind of me. I would never hurt anyone...except myself."

I'm poised in the doorway, ready to run, but hesitate. "What do you mean about hurting yourself?"

"It's a sickness, my compulsion to steal. When I see something pretty like this shaker, I have to hold it." When he lifts the crystal it catches light from the ceiling lamp and glitters like a handful of diamonds. "Next thing I know I've taken it. I don't mean to steal, but it happens. My therapist is helping me with my kleptomania but sometimes I lose control."

"You stole the pepper shaker because you're sick?"

He nods. "I feel remorse afterward and return what I've taken. But when I heard you tell Sergei the pepper shaker was stolen by an animal, I panicked because it was in my pocket. No one knew I had it, and I was terrified my uncle would find out. He wouldn't understand about my...my sickness. He can be a very unforgiving man."

"So why not return it to the kitchen? Why bring it to Angel's room? Did you want her to be blamed for the theft?"

"No! I'd never do anything to hurt her." He hangs his head, ashamed. "I've been trying to get into the kitchen all morning—but your father is there. I knew it would be safe in Angel's room. Please, don't tell anyone. Give me time to return the shaker to the kitchen."

He has the same pathetic expression Leo gets when an invention breaks or isn't working properly. What harm can there be in letting him return the pepper shaker? My dad will be thrilled to have it back. If only getting the emerald king back was as easy. A new suspicion jumps into my head.

I frown at Irwin. "I'll keep a secret if you tell me the truth."

"About what?"

"You admitted to stealing the pepper shaker, which makes me wonder what else you might have taken." I look him squarely in the eyes. "Do you have the emerald king?"

"Of course not! I wasn't even here when it happened!" He looks so shocked that he's either a good actor or telling the truth. "I wouldn't be working for my uncle if the boy hadn't stolen it."

"RJ," I say in a whisper, not wanting to believe that a kid who created a club to help animals could also be a thief.

"Yeah, RJ took it." Irwin nods. "My uncle felt so betrayed he forbid any mention of my cousin Deidra or her son. He said they were dead to him." Irwin's voice breaks. "And now I've betrayed my uncle. He'll send me away too if he finds out."

"He won't find out from me," I say solemnly. "As long as you swear you're going to return the crystal shaker."

"I will." Irwin blows out a shaky sigh. "And I'm sorry for hurting your arm. I shouldn't have grabbed you. Is there anything I can do to make it up to you?"

"Yes." I hold out my hand. "The key to the wine cellar, please?

"Oh, that. Here," he says as he reaches into his pocket.

The old-fashioned key is heavy iron with scrollwork at the top and jagged teeth at the bottom—perfect for a dungeon door.

When I rejoin Sergei, Becca, and Leo in the foyer, Angel is there too. Her glitter lashes flutter in surprise like she just found out there's a ferret thief loose in the castle.

"I've got it!" I wave the key. "Irwin gave it to me."

"Why didn't he come back with you?" Angel's purple hair spills over her angel-winged shoulders as she looks up the curved staircase.

"He has…um…some important work to do," I say awkwardly.

"What's more important than finding the animal who's been stealing my things?" She holds up the ragged sequined scarf. "I can't believe a wild animal is loose in the castle. I'm absolutely flubbergasted."

Leo frowns, and I know it's because "flubber-gasted" isn't a real word.

"What if it attacked me while I was sleeping?" Angel shudders.

"Ferrets aren't dangerous," Becca assures her calmly.

"Easy for you to say—you don't live in this ferret-infested castle." Angel dramatically sweeps her arms to take in the whole castle. "No wonder Mr. Bragg loses pens so often. I saw at least three pens in that nest in Sergei's shed. My halo was there too, but it was so filthy I may never be able to wear it again."

"Bandit...the ferret...won't take anything else," Becca says in a calming tone. "If we can't catch her ourselves, my mother runs the Wild Oak Animal Sanctuary and will bring a team of volunteers to help."

Leo taps his tablet. "The target is stationary in the cellar."

"She's probably sleeping and will be there for a long time," Becca guesses. "Ferrets sleep fifteen to twenty hours a day."

"So what are we waiting for? I have the key, so let's go to the cellar and—"

"What do you want in my wine cellar?" a deep voice interrupts.

King Bragg steps out into the foyer, striding purposefully over to us. He wears a denim vest over a white shirt with a whimsical music-note patterned tie. "If you're having a party," he says wryly, "why wasn't I invited?"

"Not a party, sir." Sergei dips his head as if embarrassed. "There's a ferret in the wine cellar."

"Sergei, these kids are playing a prank on you." King Bragg pats his housekeeper on the back. "This is all very amusing, but I'm preparing for a conference and have no time for this nonsense. You children go along home."

His condescending tone makes me so mad I blurt out, "But Bandit *is* in the cellar! And she's not really a wild animal. She belonged to your grandson. She wouldn't steal stuff if he hadn't abandoned her."

King Bragg stiffens like a suit of armor. "I don't have a grandson."

"Yes, you do, and his name is RJ! He used to live in our cottage until you kicked his family out." I've gone too far, but I can't stop now. "He nursed the ferret and other animals back to health. He probably played with Bandit in the castle, and that's why she keeps coming back to look for him. I don't know why he left her behind or why he stole the emerald king." A thought suddenly strikes me. "...Or maybe he didn't steal it! Maybe Bandit could have taken an emerald chess piece—"

"Like the ferret could have taken the missing pepper shaker?" interrupts Angel.

I frown. "We may never know everything Bandit took," I say, not wanting to rat on Irwin. "But that means RJ isn't guilty! And he—"

"*Kelsey!*" thunders a voice I know too well.

My dad's face is furious as he steps into the foyer.

I cover my mouth with my hand as if I could shove my words back inside.

"What's this about a pepper shaker?" Mr. Bragg strides over to my father. "Is she referring to my crystal and diamond pepper shaker?"

Dad, who always seems tall and powerful to me, withers under his employer's accusing gaze. "Yes, Mr. Bragg."

"A valuable object was stolen from my kitchen and you didn't bother to inform me?" Mr. Bragg's anger echoes off the walls.

When my father hangs his head and nods, King Bragg turns back to us. "You children will leave now."

There's no point in arguing. Even if I hadn't promised to keep Irwin's secret, no one would believe me now. By losing my temper, I've lost my chance to search for the ferret, and I may have lost my father his job.

"I'll talk to you at home, Kelsey," Dad adds in a tight, controlled voice.

By tomorrow my family may be homeless.

- Chapter 25 -

King, Queen, Pawn

Leo, Becca, and I don't say much as we trudge down the stairs. The sky is full of stormy-dark clouds stealing the sunlight. I shiver as a chill wind whips through my clothes, and I wish I had my jacket.

Leo's blond hair sweeps across his forehead as he pauses on the circular driveway to study his tablet. "The signal keeps fading in and out but the red dot is still in the cellar."

"Lot of good that does for us," I say bitterly. "I never should have mentioned RJ or the pepper shaker. Why don't I ever think before opening my big mouth?"

"You were telling the truth." Becca squeezes my hand. "Mr. Bragg should have believed us. But he's so puffed up with pride about everything that belongs to him. Do you notice how often he says 'my'? My cellar, my castle, my nephew. And he lied about RJ. I wouldn't want him for a grandfather. I feel sorry for RJ."

I feel sorrier for me, I think in despair. There's no way my parents will let me keep Honey now. We could end up living in a no-pets apartment again and lose Handsome too. It's all my fault.

Hanging my head, I realize I'm still holding the wine cellar key.

"Oops. I forgot to give this back." I glance up at the ominous castle.

"Your dad can return it tomorrow," Becca suggests.

But will Dad still have his job tomorrow?

"I better return it now," I say with a sigh.

Becca and Leo both stare at me like I've lost my mind.

"You can't go back in there!" Becca exclaims in horror.

"It would be unwise," Leo adds, frowning.

"I'll be quick," I assure in a braver tone than I feel. "I just hope Sergei or Angel answers the door."

Becca bites her lip. "Just leave the key on the

front step."

"Where it could get lost and then I'd be in worse trouble. I better knock."

"Be careful." Becca gives me a quick hug.

Returning to the castle is terrifying. I imagine the tense conversation going on right now between King Bragg and my father. I am in so much trouble.

I rap the brass knocker but no one answers. Not a good sign. I try the doorknob and it turns easily. I guess in all the commotion, Sergei forgot to lock it behind us. Peeking inside, I see the foyer is empty.

In case I need a quick getaway, I leave the door open a crack. I tiptoe to a small table where I can leave the key.

But I pause to think about my new theory. Did Bandit, not RJ, steel the emerald king? If so, the missing emerald could still be in the castle hidden in a ferret nest. And what better hiding place than a dungeon-like cellar? Was RJ framed for a crime committed by his own ferret?

I doubt I'll find a nest or anything more valuable than wine bottles in the cellar but no one is around and I'm too curious to leave.

I hear voices rise from the study, but it's quiet in the hall leading to the cellar. Still tiptoeing like a thief, I pass the library and turn down a narrow corridor leading to the heavy door guarding the wine cellar.

The key slips into the lock, silent and swift.

Click.

A flick of a wall switch bathes rows of bottles with golden light. I move carefully down the staircase, my spy pack bulky on my back. When I reach the bottom, I survey the rows of wine bottles. I begin with the row on the right and search systematically. No sign of a nest. I search beneath the staircase and in shadowed corners. Still nothing.

The only place left to search is the cage-like wine vault. An electronic keypad flashes on the door's lock.

I press my face against the steel bars, peering past a wine rack that reaches the ceiling. It's creepy dark and dank smelling. I shake off my spy pack and pull out my penlight. I sweep the tiny beam across the vault. In the farthest corner, too far for my light, is a shadowy lump.

Could it be a nest?

A ferret can slip through the narrow bars, but I can't. Maybe I can disable the electronic lock. I'm searching my spy pack when the room goes black.

"What?" I mutter, more annoyed with the faulty lighting system than scared...at least until I hear the footsteps.

The lights suddenly burst back on.

I blink in surprise at the purple-haired girl walking down the stairs.

"Angel!" I sigh in relief. "I'm so glad it's you."

"Why are you down here?" She sounds worried as she hurries over to me. "Are you all right, Kelsey?"

I nod then point into the wine vault. "Look! I found another nest!"

"Wowtastic!" Her peach-shimmery grin fills her face.

"But I can't get inside." I point to the lock. "I don't know the electronic password."

"I do." She leans close to whisper. "Want to know a secret?"

I never turn down secrets. "What?" I ask in a hush.

"Mr. Bragg usually uses the same four numbers: his daughter's birthday." As she's speaking, Angel reaches for the electronic pad and taps quickly. A green light flashes and the door slides open.

"Go on," Angel says, pushing me forward. "Be a hero and find something amazing. I'll stand guard."

Shadows darken the far corner and it's hard to see if the dark shape is a nest. I need a better light. I open my spy pack and put on my flash cap—a baseball cap with a strong light attached.

"What else do you have in that backpack?" Angel leans in to look. "Is that a fingerprint kit? And handcuffs? What are you, some kind of kid spy?"

"I never reveal my secrets." Smiling, I slip on a pair of gloves.

The flash cap lights my way as I enter the vault. In the corner I find a pile of junk larger than the nests in the shed and tree house.

"What do you see in there?" Angel calls out.

"It *is* a nest!"

"Anything valuable?" she asks.

"I'll look." Starting from the top, I pull out a spoon, a ripped envelope, a dried banana peel, three pens, green shoe laces, and a pink sock.

"That's my sock," Angel exclaims when I hold it up to the light.

"You won't want it now. Yuck. And this looks like part of a man's shoe." I toss aside a rubber heel.

My heart speeds up when I spy something green and shiny. I reach down and pick up a…

…a tiny jade pig.

"I remember that statue—it belongs to Mr. Bragg's daughter," Angel says. "Deidra collects pig statues and every birthday her father would buy her one from his travels. Don't stop now. Keep looking."

Angel stares eagerly at me through the metal bars as if she's been waiting for Christmas and I'm Santa. "Do you think the emerald king is here?"

So she guessed this possibility too.

"I don't know," I say honestly. "But if the ferret did take it, she might have hidden it here."

"Oh, I know she took it," Angel says sharply. "I saw RJ's ferret carry it from the toy room and jump through the window to the roof."

"You knew the ferret had it instead of RJ?" I ask, puzzled.

"I thought the stupid animal gave the emerald to RJ. It wasn't until weeks later when I read Deidra's letter to her father that I realized RJ didn't have it and the ferret must have hidden it."

I try to make sense of her words. "RJ's mother wrote to King Bragg?"

"Only once—but he never saw that letter." When Angel giggles, she sounds like a little girl but there's a very grown-up glint in her eyes.

"Why didn't he get the letter?" The jade pig slips from my fingers back into the nest.

"Stop asking questions. Move aside and I'll look." Angel strides inside the vault. "It's too dark to see anything. Can I borrow this?" She plucks off my flash cap and sticks it on her own head. "This nest stinks. If I touch it, I'll probably get a million diseases."

"Want to wear my gloves?" I wiggle my gloved fingers.

"No. You can keep looking but be thorough. I'm not leaving without that chess piece." She aims the flash cap on the pile. "I'll help by shining the light."

"Ooookay," I say uneasily.

I go back to work, wondering why she's being so bossy when we both want to find the emerald to complete the chess set. I push aside ripped papers, cloth, and fur until my gloved fingers touch the floor.

"It's not here," I murmur to myself. "I was so sure it would be since this nest is closer than the one in the tree house."

"What tree house?" Angel's voice rises excitedly.

Oops, I shouldn't have said that. "Um...nothing."

"Tell me!"

"I-I can't...it's a secret." My thoughts move in slow motion, piecing together her puzzling words. She knew RJ didn't steal the chess piece but she let him take the blame. And she didn't show her boss a letter from his daughter.

I squint into the glare of my flash cap on Angel's purple head. Something isn't right. She's acting so weird...not friendly and sweet but kind of scary.

Does she want the chess piece for her boss or herself?

As I'm wondering this, Angel suddenly lunges forward. She snatches my spy pack and jumps out of the wine vault. She slams the door—locking me inside.

"Angel, what are you doing? "I run to the bars, clasping my fingers around cold metal. "Is this some kind of joke?"

"No joke."

Panic rises inside me. "Let me out!" I demand.

"I will if you tell me how to find this tree house," she says coolly.

"Unlock the vault and I'll take you there."

"Ha!" she snorts. "You'll run off and steal my emerald king."

"But why are you doing this? You're my friend.

You showed me your room and even gave me a gift." I touch the aquamarine necklace around my neck. "I thought you liked me."

"I do—but I like me more." She giggles. "It's nothing personal. I would look terrible in prison orange, so I have to leave. And I'm taking the emerald king with me."

"Why do you want it?" I ask so softly she has to move closer to hear me.

"Because it's gorgeous and—"

I make a sudden grab for her but she jumps out of range.

Smiling, she wags her finger at me. "Good try, Kelsey, but you'll have to be quicker to catch me."

"The police will catch you if you steal the emerald king," I retort.

"It was never reported stolen. I can keep or sell it and no one will care."

"But it doesn't belong to you," I say confused, even though locking me in a wine vault proves she's the opposite of an angel.

"It's not my fault I can't resist pretty things." Her sigh is heavy with self-pity. "This is the best job I've ever had. I'd really hoped to stay longer. But Irwin suspected me and searched my room until he found the crystal. He's probably telling Mr. Bragg right now. I saw him talking with you—what was that about?"

"He confessed to stealing the crystal pepper shaker."

"Poor sweet guy lied to protect me." She shrugs. "I told you he was too nice. Too bad I'm not the nice girl he deserves."

"You mean...Irwin isn't a kleptomaniac?"

"Kleptomaniac would be me," she says proudly. "Call it an obsession or an illness but when I want something, I have to take it. As a kid I learned not to count on anyone but myself. And when I take something, no one ever suspects sweet little Angel. It was just bad luck Mr. Bragg's daughter found out."

I reel back against the hard concrete wall.

"No one understands how hard it is to have a stealing addiction. It's so unfair." She pouts like a toddler. "I almost had to leave a few months ago when darling daughter Deidra was going to tattle to Daddy just because I borrowed her sapphire earrings. But I stopped her with the perfect revenge. She was always bragging about her precious son so I was going to take the emerald and ruby chess set—

RJ's favorite game—as a parting gift to myself."

It's cold in the cellar but the chills crawling up my skin have nothing to do with the temperature.

"Only that sneaky ferret snatched the emerald king and raced out the window," she gripes. "What good is a chess set with a missing king? So I got even with that goody-goody. I told Mr. Bragg I saw RJ steal the emerald king. RJ had already gone home so Mr. Bragg confronted his daughter and accused RJ of being a thief. 'Don't you trust your own grandson?' she shouted. And Mr. Bragg said, 'Return the chess piece or leave my home and don't come back!' That night, Deidra, her husband, and son moved away." Angel grins slyly. "And I made sure they didn't come back."

It was Angel all along? Pitting daughter against father and blaming an innocent boy. She played them like pieces on a chess board, using RJ, Irwin, and now me as pawns. The queen has the most power, and the king never knew he'd been checkmated.

"Where is the tree house?" Angel asks calmly, as if we're girlfriends hanging out and not enemies separated by iron bars.

I press my lips together.

"It'll get very cold in here. Someone might find you…in a day or two." Angel shrugs, my flash cap swaying on her head. "By then I'll have the emerald king and be out of the country sunning on a tropical beach. What a shame you have to stay here alone. Or you can tell me how to find this tree house and I'll let you out."

I don't believe her. She's told me too much to let me go. So I say nothing.

"Fine, stay locked up. And thanks for this nifty backpack and the cool lighted hat." She slips my spy pack over her shoulders then climbs up the staircase. At the top stair, she looks down. "I hope you're not afraid of the dark."

She turns off the light.

Chapter 26

The Mystery Name

I'm not afraid of the dark, but I don't like it much either.

Sinking to the cold floor, I wrap my arms around myself. I was right about the ferret nest but wrong about Angel. Of course I wasn't the only one she fooled. It's easy to fall for her lies because she's so cute and petite like punk-girl Barbie. And I was flattered she gave me a gift—which she probably stole from someone else who trusted her. I reach up and rip off the aquamarine necklace. Crumpling the necklace in my fist, I throw it across my prison.

I have to get out of here! I think in despair, hugging myself in the dark. I'm alone in a dungeon-cellar. I don't have my spy pack or flash cap. No one knows where I am...except Angel.

Think, Kelsey, I tell myself. *There has to be a way out.*

I feel my way over to the bars and try the lock again. Maybe I'll get lucky and hit the right combination. It's just four numbers.

But four numbers might as well be four million I realize after a lot of failed tries. I sink back to the floor, shivering.

Thin plastic gloves can't warm my icicle-cold fingers. I blow on my hands and imagine being in front of a blazing fireplace or snuggling beneath my heated blanket with my soft kitten snug in my arms. But thoughts of warmth make me colder, and I feel more alone than ever. Despair is a different kind of cold, stabbing my heart and stealing all hope.

Faint light shines from my watch but there's no comfort from watching seconds tick. And to add to my misery, I start to notice the sound of rustling behind the towering columns of wine bottles, and the corners are so dark that I can only imagine the creepy crawlies that dwell there. If a ferret can sneak in here, other creatures can too.

Rats? Spiders? Snakes?

The noises sound amplified as if the shadows

have weight and move with whispered breaths and shuffling steps. A shadow shifts from behind a wine rack, and the sounds draw closer...

I back into the wall, trapped and terrified.

"Are you here?" a voice calls out. "Kelsey?"

Jumping to my feet, I shout, "*Leo!* Over here!"

I hear footsteps approach and a bright light shines in my face. "Why are you sitting inside a wine vault?" Leo asks in a puzzled tone.

"It wasn't my idea," I say wryly. "Lower your flashlight—you're blinding me."

"This isn't a flashlight—it's a flash app on my phone."

"Just get me out of here." I rattle the bars. "We have to stop Angel from leaving with my spy pack and the emerald king!"

"Angel has your spy pack and the emerald?" He stares at me like he thinks I'm losing my mind.

"It's a long story. I'll explain after you open the door."

Leo aims the beam on the lock. "Do you know the combination?"

"If I did, do you think I'd still be here?" I blow out a shaky breath. "What I mean is thanks for coming to my rescue. How did you find me?"

"I tracked your GPF."

"My what?"

"Global Positioning Finder. I shot it in your hair when you ran off from the shed to chase Bandit. I didn't want to lose track of you."

I remember Leo raising the silver tube and yelling something I couldn't understand. When I reach up to feel my head, I find a sticky GPF. It takes three firm yanks to pull it out of my hair. I toss it at him.

Leo catches it. "Becca and I were almost to the tree house when I looked at my tablet and saw your green light go underground. It flickered on and off because the signal underground isn't strong." He gestures to his tablet sticking out from his pocket.

"But how did you get into the cellar?"

"The outside door. I couldn't squeeze through the crack like Bandit, but my latest version of the key spider opened the lock. Luckily it wasn't electronic like this." He shines his cell light on the lock.

"Forget the lock and call for help." I point to his phone. "Call 911 or Mom."

He glances down at the screen. "The signal keeps cutting out. I'll have to go outside to make the call."

"Hurry." Sinking back to the icy concrete, I wrap my arms around myself.

"I don't want to leave you," he says. "I should be able to get this open." He studies the lock. "Four numbers between zero and nine. According to my calculations, with a total of ten numbers that could be repeated, there are ten thousand possible combinations."

"Is that all?" I groan. "I'll never get out of here."

"Never is an infinite concept and illogical. But math is solvable."

Leo tilts his head as if accessing new data from his mental computer. In a way, it's like watching my dad when he's baking—a blend of concentration and inspiration.

Leo came because he was worried about me, I think with a rush of gratitude. He can be annoying sometimes but he's 100 percent a true friend. No one else knew I was in trouble but he figured out I needed help and came to my rescue. It hits me that I like him a lot...maybe more than *a lot*. But Becca is the one he likes best, and someone needs to warn him she doesn't feel the same way.

I clear my throat. "Leo, there's something I... um...should say..."

He doesn't look up from the lock. "There are approximately 9,950 more combinations to try."

"Yeah…So what I have to tell you…" I hesitate. "You and Becca are my best friends, but we don't know everything about each other."

"Maybe zeros," he murmurs then glances up at me. "What?"

"I'm trying to say that even friends who know each other really well don't know everything. We all have secrets."

He grins. "And you write them down in that book of yours."

"Not all of them," I say, wishing I could avoid breaking his heart.

"True. You still haven't guessed my middle name."

"You'll tell me if I guess right," I remind him.

"I will—in the unlikelihood that happens," Leo says confidently. "Go ahead. Guess."

I'd rather talk about names than feelings. "I tried lots of boy names—maybe it's a girl's name. Nannette, Nancy, Naomi, Neecy, Norma, Natasha—"

"Stop!" He groans like he's in pain. "Absolutely not a girl's name."

I pause to think. "Nadair, Naheem, Nate, Nash, Navarone, Nathan, Neil."

"No, no, no, no, no, no, and no."

"Nelson, Nemo, Nevan, Newt—"

"You're starting to repeat names," he says.

I throw up my hands. "But I'm running out of N names."

"It's inevitable. You will not guess ever," he says with absolute certainty.

I refuse to give up. Besides what else can I do while I'm trapped in a vault?

"Nimbus," I guess.

"That's not a name. It's a rain cloud."

"Nino, Nolan, Nye, Nuri, or Norvin."

His fingers tap the number pad as he shakes his head. "Incorrect."

"But I've tried every name I can think of!" I stomp my foot on the concrete. "I'm beginning to think you don't even have a middle name. That's it...None!"

He stares at me like I'm lightning and I just struck him. Slowly he nods.

"I'm right?" I ask, astonished. "You don't have a middle name?"

"Oh, I have one." He grimaces. "When I was born my parents couldn't decide on a middle name. Mom wanted to name me after her father and Dad thought I should be named after him. They finally decided not to give me a middle name. So when the nurse asked for my middle name, Mom answered, none—which the nurse wrote down on an official document so it became my legal name."

"Leopold None Polanski?" I grin.

He hangs his head. "Humiliating, but that's my name. Please don't tell anyone."

"I won't," I promise, pleased that he trusts me with his secret.

Leo's quiet as he works on the lock, and I think about his crush on Becca. Why did he have to go and fall for a club mate? It's going to ruin everything. And he'll be heartbroken if he sees her with Trevor.

"Leo, I really do have to tell you something." Although we're separated by bars, he's close enough to hear my pounding heartbeat.

"A secret?" he asks with a curious glance at me.

"Sort of...it's about you and Becca."

He stops working the lock. "What?"

I take a deep breath, suck in courage, then spit out the truth. "Becca likes Trevor."

"That's not a secret." He shrugs. "She's so obvious even I knew. And it has nothing to do with me."

"Aren't you heartbroken? I mean, I thought you liked Becca."

"Of course I like her."

"More than like her," I try to explain. "That day in the tree house when you wanted to tell me something, when you said you couldn't talk in front of her, well, I knew you really liked her."

"Oh, that." It's dark but even in the faint shine from his cell phone I can tell he's blushing. "Yeah, I did want to ask you something. But it wasn't about Becca…it was about you."

"Me?" I gasp.

Now I'm blushing and don't know what to say. I mean, how does a girl ask a boy if he likes her? If he says yes, and I don't feel the same way, our friendship gets awkward. If he says no, our friendship gets awkward. And just thinking about it makes me feel awkward. I really like him, but what kind of like am I feeling?

I glance away, hoping he can't see my face.

"The reason I didn't want to talk in front of Becca was that I wanted to ask you a question," Leo goes on in the most serious tone I've ever heard him use.

"What?" I brace myself because his next words could change everything.

- Chapter 27 -
Treasure Quest

"I wanted to ask you out," Leo says, and my fears rock like an earthquake.

"Ask me out?" I repeat to make sure I'm hearing right.

"Yes. You're easy to talk to, and we share many interests like science, robots, and drones. So I hoped you might like..." He rubs his forehead. "I'm saying this all wrong. Remember when you found out my real age?"

I nod. "Your mother was planning a surprise birthday party and I overheard her say you were over a year younger than me. That was weeks ago. But you haven't mentioned anything about a party."

"There isn't going to be a party. I convinced Mom to give me a different kind of birthday celebration. So she bought me tickets to the World Robot Tournament—where robots wage battle until there's only one champion. And she said I could bring a friend with me."

"Me?" I guess.

"Affirmative. But I worried Becca might be mad I asked you and not her. I waited to ask you alone... then got nervous that you'd say no."

Leo wanted to invite me—not Becca. It's crazy that I care but I do.

"I would have said yes." I smile at him through the bars.

"Really?" He grins. "You'll go with me?"

"Sure. It sounds fun. And just so you know, I never told anyone about your real age. Not even Becca knows your birth date...birth date!" I exclaim, snapping my fingers. "I just remembered that Angel told me the lock combination is King Bragg's daughter's birthday!"

"Doesn't he know he should never use a family birthday for a password?" Leo shakes his head as he taps his phone. "It'll be easy to find. I'll go outside where the signal's stronger to check. Wait here."

"Like I can go anywhere else?" The light from his phone vanishes, and I'm alone in the darkness again.

But it isn't long before he's back.

"The code is zero-eight-three-one!" Leo exclaims as he taps his fingers on the lock.

There's a click and my barred door slides open.

"I'm free!" I cry as I step out of the prison. I think of Angel getting away and I grab Leo's arm. "Now, let's go find the emerald king!"

I follow Leo around the tall wine racks to the far side of the cellar where outside light shines through the edges of a door at the top of the other staircase.

We hurry up the stairs and push through the door into chilly air that tastes of impending rain. Stormy clouds darken the sky and blustery winds whip my hair, but I hardly notice the cold. As we sprint past the garden away from the castle and through the thick trees, all I can think about is the emerald king. It has to be in our tree house—right under our noses all along. But what if we're too late and Angel has it?

Sprinkles dampen my clothes as we near the tree house. It's the only tree on the estate that is as tall as a castle turret. All Angel had to do was look up to guess which tree is dense enough to hide a tree house—and possibly an emerald.

I hold my breath as we reach the driveway curving to our cottage, afraid I'll see Angel running away with the emerald in her hand. But the only person I see is Becca, standing beneath the tree house. She's holding something that brings a smile to my face.

"My spy pack!" I rejoice. "How did you get it?"

Becca gives it to me. "Angel had it."

"She was already here?" My hopes crash.

"Yeah, and she was all smiles and hugs like we're best friends." Becca scrunches her nose. "She said you wanted me to take her to the tree house."

"I did not say that!" I argue.

"I thought so." Becca flips her ponytail over her shoulder. "So I played dumb and said, 'What tree house?' I pointed to your spy pack and asked what she was doing with it. She said you asked her to take your backpack to the tree house. That's when I knew for sure she was lying. She called it a backpack not a spy pack. So I wouldn't tell her anything, and she started to leave with your spy pack. That made me so mad that I—"

"You what?" I hold my breath.

"I grabbed the spy pack right off her shoulder." Becca grins wickedly. "She was too surprised to stop me. She may be older, but I'm taller and stronger."

Leo applauds. "Impressive!"

"I thought I'd never see my spy pack again," I say hugging it.

"Funny thing is," Becca adds with a giggle, "all the time she was demanding to go to the tree house, we were standing right under it."

"Thanks, Becca. You not only saved my spy stuff but you may have saved the emerald king." I reach for the slats. "Follow me!"

As we climb into the tree house, I tell Becca all about what happened in the cellar.

I open the trap door and rush across the room. I'm pushing the cooler aside so I can reach the nest when I hear an odd sound.

It's coming from the animal trap!

"Becca!" I point. "Your trap worked! We've caught Bandit!"

I kneel down to peer through the slats. The ferret stares at us with frightened black eyes. She's curled with her tail circling her small body like a protective shield.

"Poor baby is terrified. Let me calm her," Becca says softly, bending over to the trap. "She's been on her own for so long, it'll take a while for her to trust humans again."

"You take care of her. I'll check the nest."

Leo offers to help but I have only one pair of gloves. So he watches while I kneel down and look through the pile. Occasionally I find something worth saving: a quarter, an unscratched lottery ticket, three pens (only one works, Leo reports), two keys, and a blue rhinestone bracelet.

When my gloved fingers touch the planked floor, I groan.

The emerald king isn't here.

My disappointment is like physical pain, bleeding hope and leaving a scar. I'd been so sure the emerald king was here.

I could clearly imagine Bandit carrying the chess piece out of the toy room window and scampering off to give it to RJ. Animals have a sixth sense and know where their people are, so I thought Bandit would have brought it to this tree house. I know from the evidence left behind that RJ was here preparing for a club meeting until his mother or father told him they were leaving. And then they were gone.

From what Angel said, Deidra tried to contact her father a few weeks later through a letter. But Angel intercepted the letter and probably any email, texts, or phone calls. As King Bragg's executive assistant she could easily make sure father and daughter had no contact.

And her plan worked—until the CCSC started investigating.

But the emerald king isn't here, I think sadly. And I don't have solid proof to clear RJ of the theft. Will Angel's confession to me be enough to convince King Bragg, or will he accuse me of lying again?

"Maybe RJ really does have it," Leo says, tapping his finger to his chin, adding up the clues.

"His mother wrote that they didn't have it," I point out.

Leo arches a brow. "If you were in RJ's place, would you tell your parents?"

"I don't know," I admit, remembering how awful I felt when my parents accused my kitten of destroying my sister's homework and her shoe. "It's hard to know what to think. Most of my information came from Angel."

"And she's a big fat liar," Becca says.

Still I think Angel was telling the truth when she described Bandit taking the chess piece. So where did Bandit put the emerald?

I try to imagine every detail of that night and the sequence of events. Bandit carrying the emerald in her mouth, jumping through the window, scampering away from the castle to the person she trusted most. She had to be coming here. But then where is the emerald?

If Bandit gave the emerald king to RJ, wouldn't he tell his mother after his grandfather accused him of being a thief? Why stand by silently while his parents packed up to move? He could have simply explained what really happened and returned the emerald—unless he didn't have it.

I stare at the hole in the wall. It's small and ragged with splinters, smaller than my hand but big enough for a ferret. Moving on instinct rather than logic, I bend down to the wood floor and shove my gloved hand into the hole.

I cringe, imaging cobwebs, animal scat, and other disgusting things that are probably on the other side of the hole. I feel something solid and pull out a purple glitter pen. It probably belonged to Angel. I wonder where she is now. I should hate her but I don't. I feel sorry for her. Liking things more than people could get kind of lonely.

Frowning, I plunge my hand back into the hole. I feel the rough bark of a wide branch and reach out with my fingers. Inching along, I grasp something bigger than an acorn. My heart speeds up as I fold it into my palm.

When I bring my hand back inside, I stare at the green stone lying in my palm.

I've found the emerald king.

The Emerald King

When Becca, Leo, and I stand on the imposing castle steps a short while later, it's like déjà vu—except Becca is carrying the ferret in a cage and I'm holding tight to the emerald king.

Leo bangs the knocker three times.

The door swings open. For a moment I expect to see Angel's smiling face—until I remember she's probably long gone by now. Why stick around for a future of orange jail jumpsuits when she can sun in a bikini on a tropical beach?

Irwin does a double-take when he sees us. "What are you kids doing here?"

"Righting a few wrongs." I gesture to the ferret cage.

"There really is a ferret!" Irwin bends over to peer inside the age. "She's awfully small to cause so much trouble."

"She's an adorable little thief," Becca says fondly as she pokes her finger through the cage to pet Bandit. "We want to show her to Mr. Bragg."

"And that's not all." I dramatically lift my hand.

Irwin's eyes light up like fireworks. "The emerald king!"

"The ferret took it—not RJ. We've found out a lot of things Mr. Bragg needs to know." I look at Irwin sympathetically, thinking of his feelings for Angel. "Will you take us to Mr. Bragg?"

"Terrible idea," Irwin says, but he's grinning. "Mr. Bragg has a fierce temper. I don't know if he'll be angrier because you're back or because he was wrong about RJ. Either way, it could be interesting." Irwin opens the door wide for us. "Follow me. He's in the music room."

As we trail after Irwin, I fight the urge to run home. I dread facing Mr. Bragg again—especially when he's still angry. But he needs to know the truth.

The music room is in one of the turrets. It has tall stained-glass windows, three shimmery chrome jukeboxes, and plush leather chairs and couches.

When we enter the room, the largest jukebox is crooning mellow '50s music—one of those Elvis Presley songs Gran Nola likes so much.

The King of Resorts is so focused on the framed photograph in his hand that he doesn't notice us. He's moving his lips as if he's talking to the photo or singing to the music. His expression is sad—until he looks up and glares.

"Irwin, what is the meaning of this?" The photograph tumbles from his hand to a couch cushion as he bolts to his feet. "These kids are not welcome in my home."

"They have something interesting to tell you." Irwin stands tall and doesn't back down. He may be a little nerdy but he's not a wimp. "You'll want to hear what these kids have to say."

"I don't want to hear...what's in that thing?" He points to the cage.

"Bandit," Becca says as she lifts her arm. "Please don't shout—she's already scared. Bandit used to belong to RJ. We trapped her in the...near Kelsey's house."

Becca glances at me, clearly not wanting to give away the secret of our tree house. (Though the owner of our house probably knows it's there.)

"I told you a ferret has been stealing things," I remind him.

Mr. Bragg bends over to look into the cage and frowns at the ferret. "If she belonged to my grandson, why didn't I know?"

"Did you allow RJ to have pets in the castle?" I ask.

"Of course not," he huffs indignantly. "I have far too many valuables to allow a rodent in my home."

"A ferret is the domesticated form of the European polecat, a mammal belonging to the weasel family," Leo corrects.

Mr. Bragg puts his hands on his hips, his frown deepening. "This animal proves nothing."

"Does this?" I raise my hand to the light of the sparkling chandelier so the emerald king glitters like the valuable jewel it is.

"Where...Where did you get that?" Mr. Bragg staggers back.

I start at the beginning, leaving out the details of our tree house as I tell them about the ferret ruining my sister's homework, finding the ARC papers, visiting with Gavin, and discovering two thieves.

"Your daughter found out and was going to tell you. But Angel framed RJ for the theft and you argued with your daughter. When your daughter moved away with her family, Angel made sure you couldn't contact her."

Mr. Bragg sinks back onto the couch and picks up the framed picture. Taking a closer look, I see he's holding a family photo of a dark, bearded man with his arm around a beautiful raven-haired woman with the same brown eyes and round-tipped nose as the young boy beside her. RJ, I'm sure, but when he was only five or six. He has the same short curly black hair and wide smile as his father. They seem like a very happy family...at least when this photo was taken.

The jukebox switches to a soulful song about lost love.

"I was sure Dee would change her mind and come back," Mr. Bragg says with a crack in his voice. "I'd lost my temper with her before but she always forgave me. But you say she wrote a letter?"

I nod. "Yeah, only Angel got the letter first."

"She probably shredded it." Mr. Bragg tightens his hand into a fist. "I trusted her with my business! I want that woman found and prosecuted. She destroyed my family!"

"She wasn't the only one at fault." Irwin frowns

at his uncle. "You accused RJ of being a thief and ordered the family off your property. You could have just asked RJ if he did it, but you assumed the worst."

Mr. Bragg sinks back into the couch, his anger fading to regret. "I shouldn't have yelled at Dee. But I didn't really expect her to leave. I tried to contact her and ask her to come back but I never heard back."

"Angel betrayed us all," Irwin says softly, patting his uncle on the shoulder. "But we need to accept blame for our actions too. I haven't been honest with you."

"Did you steal something too?" his uncle asks unhappily.

"No, but I found out Angel stole the pepper shaker, and I was going to put it back. I wanted to protect her...But she never cared about me."

"Angel fooled everyone," Mr. Bragg says sadly. "I understand protecting someone you love. Even when I thought RJ was guilty, I wouldn't report the missing emerald. I've learned the hard way how much family means to me." Mr. Bragg clutches the photograph to his chest. "If I knew where they were, I'd tell them I'm sorry."

Becca whispers to me, "We should go."

I nod, but I'm still holding the chess piece.

"This belongs to you." I offer the emerald to Mr. Bragg.

"RJ loved this little king." He looks down at the chess piece. "When he was six he said it reminded him of me. I laughed and told him he'd be the King of Resorts someday. And you know what he said?"

"Um...no," I say uneasily.

"That he didn't want to wear a crown. He'd rather be the knight so he could ride a horse." Mr. Bragg chuckles sadly. "I taught him how to play chess, and he was a quite good—checkmated me a number of times. It was a shock when Angel said he'd stolen from me...My own grandson a thief." His voice breaks. "I felt betrayed and I lost my temper...Yelled terrible things I regret. And now I've lost them all."

"We'll find them," Irwin assures his uncle.

"But what if they won't come back?"

"We can only hope they will." Irwin sighs. "And if they don't...well at least you have the emerald king. The chess set is complete."

Mr. Bragg stares at the emerald in his hand. Even dusty, it shines with green prisms. But he tosses it aside. "I'd rather have my family."

Leo, Becca, and I quietly move to the door and leave the study.

We follow the same path to the foyer. I'm eager to get out and go home.

But as Leo reaches to open the front door, I hear someone call my name.

Uh-oh! It's Dad!

When I turn to face him, he's wiping flour off his hands on his apron and glaring at me. "What are you doing here?"

I tremble under his harsh tone and forget how to speak.

"It's all very exciting, Mr. Case." Becca steps forward with a big grin as she holds up the cage. "Look what we brought."

Dad stares at the ferret like it's a unicorn. "How did you...What are you...There really is a ferret?"

"That's what I tried to tell you," I say softly.

"Kelsey, I'm so sorry." Dad smells sweet like fresh bread as he slips his arm around me. "I should have believed you."

"So I can keep Honey?" I ask hopefully.

"Of course you can." He nods. "Assuming I don't lose my job and we have to move again."

"I don't think you have to worry about your

job," I say, relieved. "Mr. Bragg won't want to lose another employee."

"Another?" Dad's brows rise. "What are you talking about?"

"You'll find out soon," I say with a mysterious smile.

Chapter 29

Club Mates

A few days later, on Sunday—the last day of Spring Break—Leo calls and says he has a surprise for me and Becca. His tone is quite mysterious and I wonder if that means he's found a new mystery for the CCSC to solve.

Leo arrives at my house dressed more formally than usual in a new navy-blue vest with brass buttons, a long-sleeved blue shirt, dark black pants, and dress shoes.

Behind him, Becca winds up the driveway on her bike. She props the kickstand and rushes over to us.

"So what's the mystery?" she asks.

"Not a mystery, a solution," Leo says with a knowing smile.

I gesture for him to come inside, but he shakes his head then strides over to the tree. "It's up there," he says.

Becca and I share curious glances then follow Leo.

He pops through the trapdoor and holds it open for us. As I climb inside, I glance over at the table and gasp—three teenagers are sitting at our table!

But actually it's their table, I realize when I recognize Gavin. RJ's hair is shorter than it was in the photo and he's as tall as his grandfather. The girl is obviously Zenobia, and Gavin was right— she's gorgeous. She holds herself elegantly as she stares back at me, twisting her thick black braid.

"Kelsey and Becca, meet my surprise," Leo says proudly. "ARC members, Gavin, RJ, and Zenobia."

"Everyone calls me Zee Zee." She leans forward gracefully like she's dancing while sitting down. "I've never been a surprise before."

"Well I'm very surprised," I admit. "I know we're just now meeting, but I feel like I already know you. I hope you don't mind that I read your club notes."

"Not at all. Gavin told us you solved one of RJ's codes too, without even using the code key." Zee sounds impressed.

"Beware the little thief," I repeat the code, realizing in a startling flash that I had the meaning wrong. "RJ, I thought your message was a warning that Bandit was the little thief. But you didn't mean Bandit, did you?"

"No." RJ regards me with a solemn expression that reminds me of his grandfather. "I wrote the code the morning Mom caught Angel wearing her sapphire earrings. Mom told me about Angel and said she was going to tell Granddad about her too. She didn't want me involved, so she sent me home."

"But you went here instead," I guess.

"To get ready for our club meeting," RJ says, nodding. "I wrote the code so Gavin and Zee could guess my secret about Angel. They knew I used to tease her for looking little—like a kid more than an adult."

"But we never had that meeting. RJ didn't know what was going on at my house," Gavin adds bitterly. "And by the time I tried to see him, his family was already gone."

RJ pats Gavin on the shoulder. "I wish I had known what you were going through. My parents took away my phone and forbid me to contact anyone."

"RJ and Gavin both shut me out," Zee says with a hurt look in her eyes.

Gavin hangs his head. "You were right about Mom being guilty, but I didn't want to believe it. When Mom confessed after she was arrested, I was too ashamed to tell you. Then we moved and it was easier not to think about my friends—until they showed up."

He points to Becca and me.

"And Leo set up this meeting after he found me online," RJ adds.

"It's the most logical method for compiling our information," Leo explains.

RJ nods. "My parents forbid me to contact my friends, but I didn't know you, so I wasn't breaking their rules to answer your emails. When I found out everything that's been going on, I told my parents and Mom called Granddad. She and Dad are at the castle right now, talking. When Granddad saw her, he started crying. That made Mom cry and even Dad cried and he swears nothing makes him cry."

"I feel like crying just hearing about it," Becca says, sniffling.

"It was great seeing Granddad again and being

at the castle," RJ says. "Granddad challenged me to a game of chess later, and I'm going to kick his butt. I've been practicing. But first I wanted to see my friends." He looks at Leo. "Thanks for finding me."

"But why wouldn't your parents let you talk to your friends?" I ask, still trying to understand everything.

"At first they were so mad at Granddad, they didn't want to have anything to do with Sun Flower," RJ explains. "But a few weeks later Mom sent a letter to Granddad but he never answered. Until Leo emailed, I had no idea that Gavin's mother had been arrested or that Angel had framed me." RJ looks at his friends. "I wanted to call but I was afraid my parents would be angry."

Becca puts her hands on her hips. "But that's no reason to abandon Bandit. How could you just leave her to fend for herself?"

"I knew Gavin and Zee Zee were coming to the tree house and would take care of her. I thought they'd find my note and know Angel was the real thief."

"But I couldn't get back here," Gavin points out. "Sergei wouldn't let me onto the estate."

"Me either," Zee Zee says angrily.

"Sergei was just following orders," I say, defending him. "He's the one who fed Bandit and let her sleep in his shed. He probably saved her life."

"I feel terrible for leaving her," RJ says. "But I couldn't take her with me. Pets aren't allowed where I live now. I guess I owe Sergei a thank-you for taking care of her."

"Sergei is a really great guy," I say. "Although for a while I was suspicious of him because he pawned something worth over a thousand dollars."

"I'll bet he needed the money for airline tickets," RJ guesses. "He's at the airport now, picking up his sister and nephews. He's been saving money to bring them from Russia for a visit."

Becca, Leo, and I exchange a look that says, "Another mystery solved." We're a great team, I think. My gaze lingers on Leo and I wonder what it will be like to go to a robot show with him.

Then Zee Zee, Gavin, and RJ tell us about the animals they found and nursed back to health. We tell them about finding kittens in a dumpster and rescuing lost animals. Becca pulls out her phone and shows them photos of Zed and the 130-year-old tortoise named Albert. When Becca holds up a photo she took that morning of the Fur Bros playing with Bandit, RJ looks sad.

"I miss Bandit, but I can't have pets in our new apartment."

"I know what that feels like," I say sympathetically. "Now we live in a house and I have both my cat and dog. Things will get better for you too. Don't worry about Bandit. Becca's mom will find a good home for her."

A little while later, the ARC kids have to leave. Their club is over, but they promise to keep in touch with one another—and us too.

"Want to go on a lost pet ride?" Leo suggests when it's just the CCSC.

Smiling, we climb down from the tree house and ride off looking for lost pets—and maybe even our next mystery.